Fashions Fade, Haunted Is Eternal

A HAUNTED VINTAGE MYSTERY

Rose Pressey

KENSINGTON PUBLISHING CORP.

www.kensingtonbooks.com

KENSINGTON BOOKS are published by

Kensington Publishing Corp.
119 West 40th Street
New York, NY 10018

All Kensington titles, imprints, and distributed lines are available at special quantity discounts for bulk purchases for sales promotions, premiums, fund-raising, educational, or institutional use. Special book excerpts or customized printings can also be created to fit specific needs. For details, write or phone the office of the Kensington sales manager: Kensington Publishing Corp., 119 West 40th Street, New York, NY 10018, attn: Sales Department; phone 1-800-221-2647.

KENSINGTON BOOKS and the K logo are Reg. U.S. Pat. & TM Off.

ISBN-13: 978-1-4967-1466-4
ISBN-10: 1-4967-1466-0

First printing: January 2019

10 9 8 7 6 5 4 3 2 1

Printed in the United States of America

Electronic edition: January 2019

ISBN-13: 978-1-4967-1467-1
ISBN-10: 1-4967-1467-9

"Prolific mystery author Pressey launches a cozy alternative to Terri Garey's 'Nicki Styx' series with an appealing protagonist who is as sweet as a Southern accent. The designer name-dropping and shopping tips from Cookie add allure for shopaholics."
—*Library Journal*

IF THE HAUNTING FITS, WEAR IT

"Cookie Chanel must investigate the horse-racing community to find a killer. . . . After *Haunted Is Always in Fashion,* Pressey's fifth amusing paranormal cozy is filled with quirky characters and fashion, along with a few ghosts. Fans of Juliet Blackwell's 'Witchcraft' mysteries may enjoy the vintage clothing references. Suggest also for fans of Tonya Kappes."
—*Library Journal*

"Haunted by three ghosts, a young woman searches for a jockey's murderer at the Kentucky Derby."
—*Kirkus Reviews*

HAUNT COUTURE AND GHOSTS GALORE

"It was a pleasure to read. I listened to this one, and I'm so glad I did. The novel is narrated by Tara Ochs. She does a fine job of narrating, keeping up the pace and differentiating voices well. The story moved right along. If you have a chance to listen, I recommend it with this one."
—Jaquo.com (on the audio edition)

Also by Rose Pressey

THE HAUNTED VINTAGE MYSTERY SERIES

If You've Got It, Haunt It

All Dressed Up and No Place to Haunt

Haunt Couture and Ghosts Galore

Haunted Is Always in Fashion

If the Haunting Fits, Wear It

A Passion for Haunted Fashion

Available from Kensington Publishing Corp.

To my son, who brings me joy every single day.
I love you.

Chapter 1

Cookie's Savvy Tips for Vintage Shopping

Remember that designer labels fetch a higher price tag.
If you're looking to save money, try finding a
similar piece that was handmade or
without the designer label.

Gnarled and twisted branches draped down over the cemetery's gates, as if they wanted to reach out and grab every person who walked through. The location for the photo shoot gave me the creeps. I wasn't sure why the photographer, Tyler Fields, had insisted on taking the photos in the spooky Sugar Creek Cemetery.

He'd called me just a week ago and said, "Cookie, I need you to style the models. We don't have time to waste, so I expect you to be ready on short notice."

Normally, I would have told him there was no way I could work with such little warning. This was a big opportunity for me though, so I'd agreed. After all, owning my own vintage clothing store, It's Vintage Y'all, in Sugar Creek, Georgia, had made me something of a vintage clothing expert. So that was how I'd found myself standing in the middle of the cemetery on a beautiful fall day.

Tyler had posed the models beside the black iron fence. Headstones and mausoleums filled the background of his photos. He stomped over to the beautiful women and showed them exactly how he wanted them to stand. The longer he waited for the models to get the poses just right, the redder his face became.

Tyler was much shorter than the models, standing on his tiptoes to reach their hair. He had sandy-brown hair that parted to the side and fell over his eyes. He didn't seem bothered by this obstruction of his view. Perhaps that was why the models' poses seemed skewed. The white short-sleeved polo shirt and olive-green cargo pants he wore hung loosely on his thin frame.

I suppose since this was for the Halloween issue of *Fashion and Style* magazine, a spooky graveyard was the perfect setting. Though that didn't make it any less scary. Seeing models photographed wearing the vintage outfits that I had picked out was a big highlight of my life. I'd never thought I'd be asked to style the models for the October issue.

Some people might find it ironic that a cemetery gave me the cold chills, considering I had a ghost attached to me and she was currently critiquing the photographer's skills.

"That pose is all wrong . . . but he didn't ask me," Charlotte said with a click of her tongue.

Charlotte Meadows was a ghost and one of my

best friends. Not to mention fashionable and a former socialite. Today she wore a silk abstract-printed belted dress by Emilio Pucci. The colors were coral, turquoise, and black, which flattered her brunette hair. The dress was short-sleeved and reached just above her knees. It was a good thing she was a ghost wearing her black Christian Louboutin heels because there was no way she would have been able to walk through the grass in those things as a living being.

Charlotte had been attached to some of her vintage clothing that I'd purchased at her estate sale. She'd been by my side ever since. Lately, it seemed as if I'd had a revolving paranormal door of ghosts in my life. Nevertheless, I was hoping my current location didn't attract a new spirit.

Tombstones and mausoleums surrounded us with etched prayers on plaques and statues of angels guarding over the dearly departed. Spanish moss hung from the tree branches like curtains. The smell of damp earth drifted on the gentle breeze. At least it was the middle of the day and not dark out. There were several models, assistants, and the photographer, so my ghost friend wasn't my only companion. I'd styled the models in sweaters, wool skirts, and walking shorts with knee socks for a perfect fall look. My favorite outfit was the head-to-toe Ralph Lauren. The plaid wool high-waist walking shorts, blue-and-green-striped sweater, and knee-high socks were all pieces from the 1980s, but looked modern and current. Some styles were timeless.

I kept the 1980s theme going by wearing a dark blue Calvin Klein shirtdress. The gold buttons down the front and the string belt with gold tassels meant accessories weren't needed with this outfit. My blue sandals were by Guess and had a canvas vamp with corkscrew sole. Charlotte said I could be one of the models, but with my height at just five-foot-two, I knew she was just being nice. Compliments from Charlotte didn't come often, so I'd take it.

We'd taken a short break, but the photographer had told the models not to get too comfortable. He had a tendency to be a bit harsh, although I'd heard he was good at his job. From the looks of the photos I'd seen in the magazine, I'd say that was accurate.

"If he barked orders at me I'd be out of here." Charlotte gestured over her shoulder. "He has the disposition of a rattlesnake with a toothache."

"Unfortunately, I think the women will put up with it just to keep their jobs," I said.

I'd only been around Tyler for a short time now, and I already wasn't fond of him. Thank goodness he wasn't yelling orders at me. Charlotte stared in the direction where Tyler stood. He was doing something to his camera lens. If I knew Charlotte, and I thought I knew her well, she was plotting something against Tyler. She enjoyed playing pranks on people when she felt they were misbehaving.

She liked to do things like knocking stuff out of their hands, touching them, or turning off lights. The usual ghostly shenanigans.

"Charlotte, don't get any ideas," I warned with a point of my finger.

She held her hands up. "What? I wasn't planning anything . . . I certainly wasn't scheming to knock the camera out of his hands. Oh, maybe I should push over that tripod."

"He's already frustrated enough. Don't push him."

Charlotte mumbled something that I couldn't understand. That was probably for the best. Movement to my right caught my attention. A man had just walked out from behind one of the tall headstones. What had he been doing back there? Where had he come from? There was only one entrance to the graveyard and that was at the front. Based on the tall headstones around him, I guessed his height at six feet. He had wide shoulders and a muscular physique. His blond hair was cut so short that he almost appeared bald. He wore black jeans, a black leather jacket, and black boots.

"Who is that?" Charlotte asked.

"That's what I'd like to know," I said. "He just came out from behind that tall headstone."

"There's something suspicious about that," Charlotte said. "We need to keep an eye on him."

I would definitely do that. The man was headed toward the group of models who were talking while taking a break.

"Do you think he has bad intentions?" I asked. "I don't like the way he is walking toward them."

"This could be dangerous," Charlotte said.

"Maybe you should alert someone," the woman beside me said.

"Yes, maybe I should." My eyes widened when I realized a stranger was standing beside us.

How had she slipped up on us? Who was she? I hated to be rude, but I wanted to know who she was.

"Who are you?" Charlotte asked with a scowl on her face.

Charlotte, on the other hand, didn't hate to be rude.

"Pardon me, my name is Minnie Lynn." Dimples appeared on her round cheeks when she smiled.

"That's nice, Minnie, but that still doesn't tell us who you are." Charlotte eyed Minnie up and down.

I scanned Minnie's appearance at that point too. Minnie didn't have to answer completely for me to know that she was a ghost. Well, I suppose I didn't know for sure, but the fact that we were standing in a graveyard and Minnie was dressed head-to-toe in vintage clothing gave me a good clue. Minnie wore a long cream-colored dress from what looked like the 1920s. A cute cloche-style hat rested on top of her head. Brown hair peeked out from underneath.

Before she got a chance to answer, yelling caught our attention. The man who had appeared from behind the headstone was now arguing with Tyler. I wasn't quite sure what they were arguing about.

"Maybe we should move closer so that we can hear better," Charlotte said.

"What if they start fighting? We should probably stay clear of that," I said.

One of the models managed to get the man away from Tyler. The model and the man walked out of the cemetery.

The photographer walked back over to the area where he'd been taking photos before the break. "All right, everyone. Let's get back to work."

His words were so harsh and he barked the orders. I had nothing else to do other than collect the clothing that I'd allowed them to borrow once the shoot was over. Now I was anxious to get out of there. I watched as the assistant raced over and adjusted the clothing on the models. Tyler stopped snapping photos and frowned at me. I attempted a smile, but he turned his attention back to the models. Perhaps he didn't want me here. Tyler snapped photos and called out orders to the models. The model who had walked the man out from the cemetery came rushing back over.

"It's about time. Get over there." Tyler barked out the command.

"I'm ready," she said, taking her place next to the other women.

Tyler didn't speak to her directly. He just snapped photos again.

"I wonder what that is all about?" Minnie Lynn said, capturing my attention once again.

Charlotte whipped her focus on Minnie once

again. She walked over to Minnie, standing right in front of her. "Now I didn't see you enter the cemetery, so who are you? Are you with the magazine?"

Minnie looked at me, as if to say *Please get this woman to leave me alone.* I was sorry, but I couldn't help her. Once Charlotte got on something she wouldn't let it go.

"Well, we are curious who you are. It's not often that we meet strangers in the middle of the cemetery," I said.

"Often? Try never." Charlotte eyed Minnie up and down.

Minnie looked down at her cream-colored pumps. There were no stains on her shoes. No signs that she'd been walking through the soft earth of the cemetery; of course there wouldn't be any if she truly was a ghost.

"I don't know why I'm here." Her voice was soft and low.

Charlotte quirked an eyebrow. "I don't believe that."

My gaze traveled from Minnie's feet to the top of her head. I took in every detail of her vintage clothing. After all, that was my job. When my eyes fell on the long strand of pearls around her neck, I knew she was here because of me. I'd recently picked up pearls at an estate sale identical to the ones she was wearing now.

"I suspect I know what's going on with Minnie."

Her big brown eyes widened. "You do?"

"Do you know that you're a ghost?" I asked.

She stared at me. "Yes, I know."

"Well, why didn't you say so? I'm a ghost too." Charlotte gestured toward herself.

Now it was Minnie's turn to eye Charlotte up and down. "I can tell."

Charlotte scowled. "What's that supposed to mean?"

"Don't be defensive. I saw absolutely no one other than Cookie look at you. That means they can't even see you."

Charlotte's expression eased. "Oh, I guess that's a good reason."

"Wait. How did you know my name?" I asked.

"I've been hanging around since you bought my necklace. I just didn't show myself until now."

I raised an eyebrow. "You have?"

"Why show up now?" Charlotte placed her hands on her hips.

Movement caught our attention, stopping the conversation. The models were walking away from the shoot and headed toward the cemetery's gates.

"What's happening, Krissy?" I asked, hoping that was her name.

Yes, now I remembered her full name—Krissy Dustin. She'd told me earlier when I'd given her the outfit. She was the model who had walked the muscular guy out.

"Tyler said he needed a break from us. I guess we weren't doing what he wanted." She pushed her blond hair away from her face.

"Where did he go?" I asked.

She pointed. "I guess he's taking a walk."

When I looked out across the cemetery, I spotted Tyler walking in the distance. He disappeared around one of the tall oak trees. Krissy joined the other models outside the cemetery.

"He'll get over it," Charlotte said with a wave of her hand. "Now back to the conversation with Minnie."

Once again, our talk was stopped when a gunshot rang out.

Charlotte gasped and clutched her chest. "Heavens to Betsy. What was that?"

Chapter 2

Charlotte's Fashionable Tips for the Afterlife

===========

*The living don't always listen. Sometimes you have
to nag them. It's completely unavoidable.*

I wasn't sure why I took off running in the
direction of where I'd heard the shot. If I'd been
thinking clearly I would have sprinted away. I suppose I was thinking someone might have wanted
my help.

Charlotte ran beside me. "Cookie, what are you
doing? You should be running in the opposite direction."

"I have to see what happened," I said as I jogged.

"This will not end well," Charlotte said.

As I neared the rear area of the graveyard I spotted one of the models running toward me. Once
she was close to me she practically collapsed into
my arms. She was a lot taller than me, so I held her
up as best as I could.

"It's terrible," she said breathlessly.

"What happened?" I asked as I held her by
the arms.

She turned her head and looked in the opposite

direction, and just pointed toward a line of trees. "Tyler." That was the only word she uttered.

"What happened to Tyler?" I asked.

"Something isn't right here," Charlotte said with a click of her tongue.

"He's dead," the model said.

The announcement hit me like a punch to the stomach.

"Why does she have blood on her clothing?" Charlotte asked.

My gaze traveled to the model's sweater. Charlotte had a good question, but I couldn't ask right now. I had to go to Tyler.

"Call 911," I said as I took off running.

When I reached the tree I almost hesitated, unsure of what I was about to see. What if he needed help? There was no time for second-guessing. I had to hurry, so pushing back my fear, I ran around the tree. Though I immediately stopped in my tracks. Tyler was only a few steps away. His lifeless body was next to a headstone.

I inched a little closer. "Tyler, are you all right?"

There was no answer.

"This guy is having a bad day." Charlotte leaned against one of the tall headstones.

"No joking, Charlotte, this is serious," I warned.

"You're telling me," she said.

"Oh dear. Is he dead?" one of the assistants asked.

"It looks that way," I said as I leaned down and checked for a pulse.

There were no signs of life. Tyler didn't move and he definitely didn't speak. I wasn't sure if I trusted the model to call 911. Maybe it was because I'd seen the blood on her. Had she killed Tyler?

I pulled out my phone and called for help. When the operator answered I gave her the location. I knew that soon Detective Dylan Valentine would be on the scene. What would he say when he realized I was witness to another murder? That was how we'd met in the first place. It probably wouldn't look good with his colleagues that his girlfriend was the witness to a homicide. As I walked around the headstone, Tyler's assistant came running over. She stopped abruptly. Tyler's legs were visible from where she stood. The rest of his body was concealed from where I stood.

"Where is Tyler?" the woman asked with panic in her voice.

I motioned behind me. "I've called an ambulance."

Her gaze followed the direction of my pointing finger. The color drained from her face. "What happened to him? Someone help him!"

"I think the coroner is needed instead of an ambulance," Charlotte said.

When the others stepped around the headstone and discovered Tyler, several of them screamed. It seemed like only seconds had passed when the sirens descended on the area. Thank goodness help had arrived. I spotted Dylan's car as it came to a screeching halt in front of the cemetery's gates. The door flew open and he jumped out. As if someone had pushed the fast-forward button, he raced through the entrance. I suppose he'd heard the call and knew I was here today. A few seconds later and our eyes met. A look of relief washed over his face.

He rushed over to me. "Cookie, what happened?"

"I think there's been a murder." I pointed toward the area where Tyler was located.

"Stay right there. I'll be right back." He raced toward the spot, weaving around the headstones.

How could Dylan look so pulled together in such high-stress situations? He looked the same whether he was walking into the coffee shop for a morning dose of caffeine or if he was discovering a homicide victim for the first time. Perhaps I looked at him in a different light than others because he was my boyfriend. However, others had to see this as well.

Chaos had taken over the serene graveyard. The models and assistants stood around in shock. Officers and detectives moved back and forth from the body to the front of the cemetery. They had pushed us out to the sidewalk and taped off the entrance. I scanned the group standing beside me, looking for strange behavior. It was evident that Tyler had been murdered. Someone in the cemetery was responsible for his death. There was no way I would stand around and let a murderer get by with something like this.

"What are you thinking about, Cookie?" Charlotte

waved her hand in front of my face. "You're being quiet, so I know that must mean the wheels are turning."

I snapped to attention. "Just thinking about who could have done this to Tyler."

"I don't think it would be hard to figure out that he probably had a few enemies. Narrowing it down will be the difficult task," Charlotte said.

"Why is that?" Minnie asked.

I clutched my chest. I'd almost forgotten about her. Why was she here?

"Tyler wasn't so nice to people," I said.

"That's unfortunate," she said around a sigh.

"It was unfortunate for the people who had to deal with him," Charlotte said.

"We shouldn't talk badly about the dead," I said.

"Are you kidding me? You talk badly about me all the time." Charlotte placed her hands on her hips.

"I do not! I point out things you do, but I don't talk badly."

"Well, you're a little snippy sometimes," Charlotte said.

"I am not," I replied.

"Ladies, no arguing in the cemetery. People are trying to rest in peace," Minnie said.

Charlotte shrugged and examined her fingernails. Sometimes she was too sensitive. Of course she said the same about me. Her personality was transferring to me.

A few seconds passed and Dylan headed over to where I stood. "Tell me everything."

"We heard a gunshot," I said.

Dylan looked around and saw that I was standing alone. "Charlotte and you heard the shot?"

"And Minnie Lynn," I added.

He raised an eyebrow. "Who's Minnie Lynn?"

Minnie waved her arms. "Here I am. It's me, Minnie Lynn."

"He can't see you, dear," Charlotte said, motioning for Minnie to stop waving.

"Why not? He obviously can see you. He knows you're here," Minnie said.

"Cookie told him about me, but he can't see me." Charlotte gestured with her hands, waving them in front of Dylan's face. "See, he has no idea that I'm here."

Dylan scrunched his face as if he sensed something around him.

"Oh . . ." Minnie said with pursed lips.

"Minnie Lynn is a ghost who appeared here in the graveyard," I said.

Dylan quirked an eyebrow. "A new ghost?"

"Yes, but that doesn't have anything to do with the murder," I said with a wave of my hand. "At least I don't think it has anything to do with the murder."

Minnie shook her head no.

"Right . . . so tell me what you saw," Dylan said, glancing around for Minnie.

Charlotte laughed. "Cookie is getting Dylan sucked into her ghostly world."

Only because the ghosts were forcing me to tell him about this craziness. How else could I explain all the weird things that happened? I'd kept this from him for quite some time. Eventually I had to tell him. Thank goodness he had accepted this. At least I hoped he really accepted it.

"We heard the gunshot. I knew right away that something was wrong," I said.

"So naturally you went right into the danger," he said.

"I think he's being facetious," Charlotte said.

"I thought someone might need my help. When I made my way around the headstone, I saw Tyler on the ground. Krissy was walking out from that area. We heard her scream."

"Her scream didn't sound genuine, if you ask me," Charlotte said.

"Did Krissy have a gun?" Dylan asked.

"Not that I saw," I said.

"I bet she hid it. We should look for it," Charlotte pointed out.

I'd have to remind her that the police would probably handle that.

"If someone shot him they had to be around somewhere," Dylan said. "You saw no one else leave the area?"

"Well, I was talking with the ghosts. Someone could have taken off in the other direction and I wouldn't have seen them."

"Okay, we'll search the area. Let me know if you

think of anything else." Dylan started to walk away, but turned to me again. "Are we still on for dinner?"

"It amazes me how he can go from talking about a murder to discussing dinner," Charlotte said.

That was part of the job. I was sure he wished it didn't have to be that way.

"I'll see you tonight." I waved, trying to act as if I wasn't freaked out.

When Dylan joined the other detectives I scanned the crowd again. Krissy and the muscular guy, who had returned to the cemetery, had been separated and were talking with detectives.

"I want to find out who that man is and why he was arguing with Krissy," I said.

"We can help you with that. Can't we, Charlotte?" Minnie said in her peppy tone.

Charlotte lifted an eyebrow. "We can?"

"Of course we can. Just as soon as the police are finished with him." Minnie flashed a bright smile.

Charlotte laughed. "Yes, I suppose we can do that."

"It looks as if the police will be here for a while, so we'll have to wait. In the meantime I have to get back to the shop. We'll figure out a way to find out more about him," I said.

Chapter 3

Cookie's Savvy Tips for Vintage Shopping

―――――――

Look for styles that are current again. Trends come
and go. Sometimes you can save a lot by finding
a vintage item that is the trend again.

A short walk and a few minutes later we'd arrived
at my shop. My store was in the historic part of
town. I'd painted the cottage-style building a soft
lavender with white trim. The inside was done in
the same colors with a crystal chandelier hanging
from the ceiling and a fabulous velvet settee that
mostly was a hangout for the ghosts in my life. Wind
Song jumped down from the front window and
strolled over to me. She rubbed against my legs
and circled around me. The cat shared its body
with my grandmother. Crazy, right? This wild
incident had happened during a séance gone
wrong. Now Grandmother Pearl gave me messages
from the great beyond using the Ouija board and
tarot cards.

My best friend Heather Sweet had been the one
who suggested using the board to communicate. At
first I'd been reluctant to try it, but now I was glad

that she had insisted. Heather owned the occult shop next door to my place. She gave tarot card and psychic readings, although she wasn't psychic. That had been her little secret for many years until she'd finally come clean with me. I couldn't believe she'd kept this secret from her own best friend. The fact that I now talked to ghosts had pushed her to reveal the truth. She gave it her best shot though. I felt bad being the one who could now talk with ghosts, considering she wanted to so badly. And I didn't even want to. Go figure.

Minnie tossed her hand up in a wave. "Hi, Grandma Pearl. How are you this beautiful morning?"

Wind Song marched over to Minnie and followed her across the room. That meant my grandmother must be in control of the body. Charlotte and I exchanged a look.

"You know my grandmother?" I asked.

"Only from hanging out in your shop for the past several days," Minnie said.

I placed my bag down on the counter. "Wait a minute. If Minnie has been here for several days, then why didn't you mention it, Charlotte?"

Charlotte lounged on the settee. "I can't keep track of all the ghosts that come and go around here."

My eyes widened. "What do you mean?"

"Just like I said, I don't keep tabs on who strolls through the portal."

"There are more ghosts here?" I looked around the room.

"They come and go," Charlotte said with a dismissive wave of her hand.

"And you never mentioned this? This is unsettling news," I said.

"If it was someone bad I would surely mention it," Charlotte said.

"Oh dear, I didn't mean to cause a fight," Minnie said.

"We're not fighting," Charlotte said. "Cookie's just being overdramatic . . . as usual."

"I'm going to act like I didn't hear that." I pouted.

"Go right ahead." Charlotte studied the fuchsia-colored polish on her fingernails.

"Where do the ghosts come from?" I asked.

"From the storage room. I guess with the repeated use of the Ouija board you opened up some kind of portal to the other side." Charlotte held up her hand. "Do you like this color?"

"What?" My voice raised several levels. "How do I stop it? I don't want that."

"I don't know. I'm not a paranormal expert." The bell above the door jingled, announcing someone's arrival. Charlotte said, "Here comes the expert now. Ask her."

"I definitely will ask her," I said.

"Ask me what?" Heather bounced across the floor with a spring in her step.

Apparently she hadn't heard about the murder.

Heather was my best friend, but Charlotte liked to claim that she was now my new best friend. However, Heather had been my friend longer, so she got to keep the title. With the craziness surrounding me I wasn't sure Heather wanted to be my best friend anymore. Today Heather wore a long white linen skirt, brown woven sandals, and a blue tie-dyed T-shirt. Her blond hair was pulled back into a braid. Honestly, sometimes I wondered if we'd been switched at birth and my mother was actually Heather's mother.

"Where do I start?" I blew the hair out of my eyes.

"You seem stressed." Heather leaned against the counter.

"Yes, you could say I'm stressed. Where do I start?"

"From the beginning," Minnie answered.

Heather furrowed her brow. She turned her attention and focused directly on Minnie. Minnie watched her back.

Heather looked at me. "Who is she?"

My eyes widened. "You can see her?"

Charlotte popped up from the settee and hurried over.

Heather made eye contact with Charlotte. "I didn't know you had customers."

Heather was looking right at Charlotte.

"She can see me," Charlotte said.

Heather turned to me and gave a look as if to say, "Has that woman lost it?"

"Heather, can you see both of them?" I asked.

Heather pointed at Minnie and Charlotte. "Both of these women, yes."

"Heather, they're ghosts," I said. "The one with the scowl is Charlotte."

Charlotte touched her forehead, ever worried about wrinkles.

Heather's mouth dropped open. "What's happening? Why can I see them?"

"I don't know. Take a deep breath." I raced around the counter and took Heather by the arm.

I knew how frightening it was to see a ghost for the first time. It was something never to be forgotten.

Heather clutched the side of the counter. I guided her over to the settee. "Here, have a seat."

"She couldn't see the ghosts before and now she can. This is amazing," Minnie said.

Heather stared at Minnie.

"Heather, this is Minnie. I met her in the graveyard this morning." I gestured.

That sounded so strange when I repeated it out loud. I was glad no customers were in the store to hear that.

"Why is she here?" Heather asked, looking Minnie up and down.

"I'm not sure yet. Why are you here, Minnie?"

Minnie tossed her hands up. "Beats me."

"Okay, never mind that right now. There is something else I need to tell you," I said.

Heather rubbed her temples. "More ghosts?"

"More murder," Charlotte said.

Heather gasped. "Murder? Who?"

"Tyler Fields, the photographer for the photo shoot. Someone killed him in the cemetery this morning." I hated to sound so blasé about it, but those were the facts.

"Do they know who did it?" Heather asked.

"Not yet. I saw one of the models run from that area right after it happened. She screamed and acted shocked when she found his body."

"She claims to have found the body. She could have murdered him," Charlotte said.

"Do you think she has a reason to murder him?" Heather asked.

It was strange watching Heather talk directly to Charlotte. No longer did I have to be the go-between in their conversations. Though that might be a bad thing. There were a lot of comments from Charlotte that I didn't relay to Heather. It would only cause an argument.

"That's what I intend to find out," I said. "In the meantime, why do you think you can see the ghosts?"

Heather looked Charlotte up and down. "Charlotte, you look exactly how I imagined you would. Of course I've seen pictures, but that doesn't give you a true image of the person."

Charlotte quirked an eyebrow. "Well . . ."

I held my breath, hoping that Heather wouldn't say the wrong thing.

"You're gorgeous."

Charlotte waved her hand. "Oh pshaw. Why, thank you, Heather."

Was Charlotte actually blushing?

"Seeing you is much more accurate. Since you don't have the scowl in the photos." Heather pointed at Charlotte's face.

Charlotte glared at her.

Heather turned her attention to Minnie. "And you are as pretty as an angel."

Minnie's smile spread across her face, lighting up her blue eyes.

Heather leaned back in the settee. "I have no idea why I can see the ghosts now. I did nothing different."

"That is odd," I said. "I would say it's a good thing to see and talk with the ghosts, but I'm not so sure."

"Hey . . ." Charlotte placed her hands on her hips.

"Besides you all, of course," I added with a smile.

When a customer entered the shop, Heather and I stopped our conversation with the ghosts. As I stood next to the rack of dresses helping the customer, I caught movement out the window. Krissy and the guy from the cemetery were standing on the sidewalk across the street. They were having another heated discussion. He seemed to be unhappy all the time, at least on the occasions I'd seen him. What was going on that made him so unhappy?

"Which skirt would work better with this blouse?" the woman asked, snapping me back to attention.

She held up a dark, golden-colored, quilted satin

circle skirt from the 1950s. It had a side zipper with two hook clasps.

"That's one of my favorites," I said, still somewhat distracted.

I'd almost decided to keep the skirt for myself. After reaching over to a different rack, I pulled a top off the rack. The white short-sleeved blouse had a fitted waist and tiny buttons up the back.

"This would be perfect." My gaze traveled back to the window.

"Oh, I love it." She took the hanger from me.

"What is so interesting out there?" Charlotte asked.

Minnie and Charlotte had now moved over to the window and were peering outside. Wind Song had sat up on the windowsill and was staring too.

The customer paid no attention to my distraction. She'd moved on to another clothing rack. I surveyed the items the woman was holding up. Though my attention on the clothing was short-lived. I had to see what the couple did next.

"I think the pink blouse would look nice with the skirt. What do you think?" the woman asked.

I didn't even look at the woman when she spoke. "It would look lovely."

My current customer service skills were out the window. Literally. The couple fought some more. He grabbed her arm and she yanked it away. I seriously contemplated calling the police. I hadn't liked the way he grabbed her arm. He seemed as if he was trying to get her to stay. He needed to accept if she wanted to leave.

"I'll take both outfits," the woman said.

Somehow in spite of my bad sales pitch I'd sold the items. I watched as Krissy marched down the sidewalk. The guy got into a car and took off in the opposite direction. At least he'd left her alone. This left me with a bad feeling though. I definitely needed to check into it more.

Chapter 4

Charlotte's Tips for a Fabulous Afterlife

---

*Don't settle for the backseat
when you can ride shotgun.*

The day had been busy with customers. Of course that made me happy, but the ghosts had been anxious for me to find out more about the guy we'd seen with Krissy. I had to admit I wanted to know more about him as well. Something about him sent a shiver down my spine. I suppose it was because he'd seemed like such a bully.

Dylan had been busy with the murder case. So far I hadn't been able to get any information from him. I hoped that changed soon. I finished some of my paperwork and shut off the lights. Heather had a few readings tonight, so she wouldn't be able to go anywhere with me until later. The ghosts, however, were already waiting by the car as I locked the shop's door. As soon as I reached the car, the ghosts hopped in. Apparently Charlotte had already warned Minnie that she got to ride in the front passenger seat because Minnie sat in the back. I slid behind the steering wheel and turned on the engine.

Fuzzy dice dangled from the rearview mirror. This set of wheels was my pride and joy. My grandfather had left it to me. The shiny chrome glistened in the sunshine. The leather seats felt like butter.

"Such a beautiful car you have." Minnie ran her hand along the leather seat. "So modern."

Charlotte laughed. "It's a 1948 Buick."

"Oh . . ." Minnie said with pursed lips.

"Well, that is modern for her," I said.

"Where are we going first?" Charlotte asked.

I tapped my fingers against the steering wheel in rhythm with The Platters singing "Only You." Not only did I dress in vintage and drive an old car, but I listened almost exclusively to the oldies as well. Not everything in my life was retro, but a great deal of it was. Even my house was decorated with vintage items, although I liked to mix old with the new.

"Town sure has changed a lot." Minnie peered out the window in awe of the scenery.

"I wish I'd seen it back in those days," I said.

"All the buildings were here," she said.

I cruised down the main street of town. Seeing the old brick buildings restored and full of businesses made my heart happy. Flowers in the large planters along the sidewalks clung to the last days of warmth before the cooler weather set in. A banner hung high above the street announcing the upcoming fall festival. There was a hayride that I was particularly looking forward to. Not to mention Dixie Bryant's apple cider. Dixie owned Glorious

Grits. That was the diner in town. It was one of my regular stops.

"Hello? Are you listening to me?" Charlotte snapped her fingers, bringing me back to the current conversation.

"What did you say?" I asked.

"You never answered about where we're going first," Charlotte said.

"Well, since I don't know that guy's name I suppose I will have to find that out first. I can't find him if I don't know his name." I made a left turn.

"No, you cannot." Charlotte agreed.

"How do you do that?" Minnie asked.

"I'll talk with Krissy Dustin. I'm sure Dylan has instructed everyone not to leave town," I said.

"But you don't know where she's staying," Minnie said.

"It's a small town. Finding anyone is never that difficult. Especially a gorgeous model."

"Why don't you just ask Dylan where she's staying?" Charlotte asked with a sheepish smile.

"I doubt he wants me involved in the investigation, which means he'll keep all this information tight-lipped." I mimicked zipping my lips. "So don't even suggest that I should ask."

"I already suggested," Charlotte said.

"I thought I'd go by all the hotels and check. There are only three in town." I made a right turn at the light to head away from the historic section.

"Don't forget there are two bed-and-breakfasts now," Charlotte said.

"That seems like a lot of hard work," Minnie said around a sigh.

"Like Charlotte always says . . ."

"Hard work pays off." Charlotte finished the sentence for me.

"Where do you start?" Minnie asked.

"I guess I'll ask the first hotel I come to. Which is the Red Rose Inn just down the road." I gestured.

"Keep your hands on the wheel," Charlotte warned with a wave of her finger.

"This is exciting." Minnie bounced in the seat.

Charlotte raised an eyebrow. "Easily amused, isn't she?"

A couple minutes later I turned into the inn's parking lot. I'd barely parked the car and shut off the engine when I spotted him.

"Whoa, isn't that him?" I pointed across the parking lot.

"That's him, all right. I'd recognize that bully anywhere," Charlotte said.

"What will you do now?" Minnie asked.

"I suppose I could start up a conversation." I pulled the keys from the ignition.

"Like what? Oh, did you see that murder today? How about this weather?" Charlotte quipped.

"Okay, I know this is a delicate situation." I tapped my fingers against the steering wheel. "I'll have to come up with something quickly."

"What is he doing anyway?" Charlotte asked.

"He's looking around. Maybe he's waiting for someone," I said.

No sooner had the words left my lips than a couple guys approached the man. They talked for a few minutes until Krissy's friend walked into one of the rooms and slammed the door. One of the men he'd been talking to held his hands up in frustration, as if he couldn't believe the guy had stormed off.

"Wow, that was something. Too bad they didn't punch him," Charlotte said.

"Oh, Charlotte. Be nice," I said.

"Now we have to know what that's all about," Charlotte said.

I opened the car door. "Yes, we do."

The men stood there for a moment. I guess to see if the other one would come back out of the room. After a few seconds they turned and started to walk away. I hurried across the parking lot to catch up with them.

"This is so exciting." Minnie hurried along beside me. "I never thought I'd get to do something like this."

"Hang with Cookie and you'll get into all kinds of trouble," Charlotte said.

As we rushed toward the men, I said, "You are half the reason I get into trouble."

"I meant that in the best way possible," Charlotte

said in her syrupy-sweet voice. "And you admit I am only half the reason."

We were now behind the men. I had to say something. They were muscular and tall. They towered over me, which meant they were a little intimidating.

"Excuse me. Can I get directions?" I called out.

"Oh dear, this will not end well." Charlotte massaged her temples.

As if ghosts got headaches. She was *so* dramatic.

The men turned around, briefly eyeing me up and down.

"We're not from around here, so I'm not sure if we'll be of much help," the bigger of the men said.

"I could have told you that would happen," Charlotte said.

I had to think of something quick.

"What are you looking for?" the other man asked.

"Cookie, you look like a deer with its eyes caught in the headlights," Charlotte said.

"Say something," Minnie urged.

"Say anything," Charlotte added.

"Just looking for Glorious Grits," I said.

Charlotte groaned. "Glorious Grits? That's what you came up with? Have I taught you nothing?"

The men exchanged a look.

The taller one said, "Sorry, never heard of it."

They turned to walk away.

"Do something." Charlotte gestured.

"This is making me nervous," Minnie said.

"That man you were talking to. Is his name Derek? If so, I bet he knows how to find the place." I rushed my words.

Minnie and Charlotte groaned. Charlotte was already rubbing off on Minnie. Hey, it was the best I could come up with under such pressure.

"No, his name is Darrin Silva," the bigger guy said.

"Well, at least you have his name now. That's a start," Charlotte said.

"He's not from around here?" I asked.

The guy studied my face, as if he were suspicious. "No, his girlfriend is in town for a modeling thing."

"Oh, so he's a model too?" I pressed.

The men laughed.

"Nah, he just likes to follow her around."

"I saw that he seemed upset," I said.

The man gave me that suspicious look again.

"You're digging a deeper hole," Charlotte said. "Maybe you should stop while you're ahead."

"I was walking through the parking lot and he caught my attention," I said. "It was hard not to notice."

"Okay, that's better. Keep this up and you might actually get somewhere," Charlotte said.

"Yes, good job, Cookie," Minnie added.

"Yeah, he has a temper. I guess that's why Krissy wanted to break up with him," the other guy said.

"Now you've got them talking; keep it going." Charlotte motioned.

"Krissy is his girlfriend? I guess he would be upset if she wanted to break up with him," I said.

"Yeah, but it's no surprise she wanted to dump him."

The men looked at each other.

The bigger guy shoved his hands into his pockets. "He's a possessive guy. I guess he thought Krissy was cheating on him with this photographer guy."

"Aha! Now we're getting somewhere. A motive for murder." Charlotte punctuated the sentence with a jab of her finger.

I wondered if these guys knew about Tyler's murder. They had to know since it was plastered all over the afternoon newspaper. It had made the news in all parts of Georgia. Soon we'd be called Murder Creek instead of Sugar Creek.

"Are you good friends with Darrin?" I asked.

"No, we just know him because of our girl-friends."

"So you're here with your girlfriends too?" I asked with a quirked eyebrow.

I guess the guy realized what I was thinking.

"Yeah, but this is a one-off. We don't usually follow them around like Darrin does."

"He seems honest. I believe him," Charlotte said.

That was shocking. She never believed anyone.

"Good luck on finding the place you're looking for. Glistening Grits?" the guy asked.

Charlotte laughed. "I'd like to see glistening grits."

"Glorious Grits," I corrected.

"Right. Well, good luck." The guy tossed his hand up in a wave and they turned to walk away.

"At least you have a name now," Minnie said.

"Yes, and I hope I find out more," I said.

I walked away from the area where I'd been standing while talking to the men, but I couldn't help peek over my shoulder several times. They hadn't bothered to look back at me, so I suppose they weren't suspicious of my questioning. That was a good thing. I'd hoped to spot Darrin again though. With his temper, maybe it was best if I didn't have any interaction with him. I was concerned for Krissy's safety. I'd have to speak with Dylan about that. I'd tell him I'd seen them arguing, but I'd leave out the part about coming to this hotel.

"Is that all you're going to do here?" Charlotte asked.

"I'll speak with the hotel manager. She's been into my shop before, so maybe she'll provide me with more information. I assume if Darrin is here Krissy is with him also," I said.

"Unless she dumped him, which is what she should have done," Charlotte said.

Chapter 5

Cookie's Savvy Tips for Vintage Shopping

———

Look for items that are being sold in a bundle.
You might find a hidden gem.

When I stepped inside the hotel lobby, I was relieved to see the manager behind the counter. The décor of this place looked like it hadn't changed since the 1950s, which was fine with me. Upholstered, teal-colored chairs with chrome legs and a kidney-shaped coffee table sat in the far corner of the room. The manager reminded me of Grandma Pearl when she was younger. Well, at least from the photos I'd seen of my grandmother when she was younger. The resemblance was definitely there.

Nancy Klondike had dark hair cut into a short bob style that reached just below her chin. Nancy ran a lot, so she had a lean, athletic build. She probably stood at five-foot-five. She immediately cast a look of surprise when I entered. I bet she wasn't used to seeing locals around here. Well, maybe a few who wanted to remain discreet.

"How can I help you, Cookie?" she asked.

"Well, at least she remembered your name," Charlotte said as she walked beside me. "That's definitely a plus for you."

Charlotte was to my left and Minnie on my right. They stared at Nancy expectantly.

"Good afternoon, Nancy." I scanned my surroundings. "I suppose you heard about the tragic event that took place in Sugar Creek."

"At least you got right to the point. Though you might try easing into it next time," Charlotte said.

If I eased into it she would have told me to get to the point.

Nancy's expression changed. Never mind that I had been right in the middle of that tragic event. People in town would be talking about that. I pressed on though since there was nothing I could do about it. I had nothing to lose at this point, right? Okay, I could be chased out of town, and my boyfriend could break up with me. That was all a bit paranoid thinking. None of that would happen . . . I hoped.

If Nancy had a hint of a smile on her face before, it had completely faded now. "Yes, I've heard. You were there at the time?"

"She knows you were there," Charlotte said.

"Nancy hasn't asked her to leave though," Minnie said.

"That's because she just wants you to tell her every little detail so she can gossip to everyone else in town." Charlotte tapped her fingers against the counter.

Nancy studied my face, as if anxiously awaiting

the details of the crime. Now I had my suspicions that she did want to gossip behind my back. Though I didn't always admit it, Charlotte was often right. She read people well.

"I was at the photo shoot providing my assistance with the vintage clothing, but I didn't see the murder actually take place. Anyway, is there a model named Krissy Dustin staying here?" I wanted to control the conversation and not let Nancy question me.

"I can't give that information." She stared at me.

Couldn't she give me the info? She obviously knew that I knew.

"She can't give you the info, but she wants to talk." Charlotte pointed at Nancy. "Ask her again."

"I know you can't tell me which room, but is she staying here?" I pressed.

Nancy looked around as if someone might over-hear. As far as I knew we were alone in the lobby.

Nancy sighed and said, "She was staying here with her boyfriend, but she left right after the murder. I think she went to stay at the bed-and-breakfast down the road."

"Thank you," I said.

"That must mean that the boyfriend has some-thing to do with the murder," Nancy said with determination.

"I suppose the police will figure that out. Thank you again, Nancy." I turned toward the door.

"Good job, Cookie," Charlotte said. "Now let's get to that bed-and-breakfast."

"Cookie is a good detective," Minnie said as she followed me out the door.

We rushed into the car and I pulled out onto the street.

"Nancy might be on to something. The fight that we witnessed. Plus, Krissy leaving the hotel could be because she knows Darrin murdered Tyler. I mean, would you stay with someone you thought was a murderer?" I asked.

"I wouldn't," Minnie said from the backseat.

Charlotte chuckled. "I agree with Minnie."

A short distance down the road and I arrived at the bed-and-breakfast. With any luck, Krissy would speak to me about the murder and why she'd had a fight with Darrin. I pulled the car up the pebbled driveway and shoved it into park. Charlotte and Minnie had already gotten out of the car and were waiting for me by the front door. Apparently they were anxious. Unfortunately, my movements weren't as swift as the ghosts'. The old Victorian house sat on several secluded acres with tall oak trees providing lots of shade. A wraparound porch invited guests to sit and sip iced tea on a hot day. Rocking chairs and several planters full of flowers decorated the porch.

Once out of the car and over to the porch steps, Charlotte said, "You know, if my boyfriend had been as possessive as those guys say Darrin was, I would have broken up with him a long time ago."

Charlotte had little patience for games. I agreed

though. Darrin would have a restraining order against him faster than he could say "jail time."

"I hope she's here," I said as I walked up the steps and to the front door.

Charlotte took a seat in one of the rocking chairs on the porch. She pushed it back and forth. To anyone else it looked as if the chair was moving on its own. I had just raised my hand to knock when someone from behind me gasped. When I spun around, I saw Krissy standing at the bottom of the steps staring at the moving rocking chair.

"Oops," Charlotte said, stopping the movement.

Krissy's eyes were wide. "I knew this place was haunted."

How would I explain this?

"Did you see that?" Krissy asked.

"See what?" I asked.

"Cookie, you're going to let her believe you didn't see that?" Charlotte rubbed her index fingers together in a shaming motion.

It was better than telling Krissy that two ghosts were on the front porch with me.

Krissy pointed at the chair. "It was moving as if someone was sitting in it."

Charlotte got up from the chair.

"It was probably the wind," I said.

Krissy glanced around at the still tree branches. Not a single breeze around.

"You're a terrible liar," Charlotte said.

"This isn't the first thing that's happened around

here." Krissy rubbed her arms, as if fighting off a chill.

"Oh, find out what else she's witnessed. I'm curious," Minnie said. "I love ghost stories."

"Yes, all we need now is a campfire and marshmallows to roast," Charlotte said drily.

Before I had a chance to speak, Krissy asked, "What are you doing here? I gave all the clothing back."

"She's a real peach, isn't she?" Charlotte folded her arms in front of her waist.

Krissy's attitude was a bit snippy.

Moving down the steps, I closed the distance between us. "Actually, I came to speak with you."

She studied my face. Usually I read people well, but she was hard to gauge. Would she speak to me about the murder?

"About what?" She crossed her arms in front of her.

Already she was on the defensive. That didn't bode well for me. Charlotte and Minnie stared with wide eyes, waiting for Krissy's reaction, when I finally revealed my reason for the visit.

"First, I'd like to say I'm sorry for what you encountered at the photo shoot. That must have been terrible," I said.

"Good idea, Cookie. Befriend her. That way she'll be more likely to talk with you," Charlotte said.

I wasn't sure she would be more likely, but I figured it was worth a shot. Maybe if I had been a bit more aggressive she would have felt pressure to talk. No, it was probably best to be nice.

Krissy tucked a strand of blond hair behind her ear. "Yes, it was traumatic."

"She doesn't seem that upset." Charlotte eyed Krissy up and down. "Her attitude is sort of flippant about the whole thing."

"Did you see anyone when you went back there?" I asked. "Maybe someone . . . other than Tyler's body, of course."

"Don't you think I would have said something if I did?" Krissy narrowed her eyes.

"Whoa. Why so defensive?" Charlotte asked.

"Perhaps she needs a cup of tea to calm her nerves," Minnie said.

"A big cup," Charlotte added.

"She must be hiding something," Minnie said. "I just realized something . . . what if she killed the man? That means we're standing here with a murderer. Maybe you should leave, Cookie; this doesn't seem like such a good idea, after all."

"You're just now realizing this, Minnie? Cookie knows how to take care of herself. Don't you, Cookie?" Charlotte said.

The ghosts were getting way too worked up. With all the chatter, I could barely remember why I'd come to talk with Krissy in the first place. Did I know how to take care of myself around a murderer? Something told me it wouldn't be as simple as running away if Krissy decided to come after me.

"Krissy, I saw you arguing with your boyfriend.

Once while at the photo shoot and again out in front of my shop. Why were you arguing?" I asked.

She glared at me. "Why is that any of your business? What are you, a detective? Are you stalking me?"

"I'm just a concerned citizen," I said. "And no, I'm not stalking you."

"You have a right to be concerned," Charlotte said. "You live in this town and don't want people going around murdering others. Though it probably does seem as if you are stalking her a bit."

Krissy crossed her arms in front of her chest. "If you must know, he's just jealous."

"It seems as if she might actually want to talk about her dilemma with this guy," Charlotte said.

"She could be under a lot of stress because of him. However, she could be the killer too," Minnie said.

"Is that why you broke up with him?" I studied her face.

"How do you know that I broke up with him? Have you really been following me?" Krissy asked, stepping back a bit. "You *are* stalking me."

"No, I am not stalking you, but I have connections in town and I know these things," I said.

"Now you really have her freaked out," Charlotte said.

"Why was your boyfriend mad at Tyler?" I asked.

"He just thought I was seeing Tyler," Krissy said.

"Were you?" I pressed.

"No, I wasn't seeing him. Darrin and I had nothing to do with Tyler's death. Do you think I would have done something right there with everyone around?"

"Is she saying she would have if we weren't around?" Charlotte asked. "Someone killed the man and she was right there."

"Darrin seemed mad enough to kill if I remember correctly," I said.

"Just because he was upset doesn't mean he would kill anyone," Krissy said.

"Doesn't mean he wouldn't either," Charlotte said with a click of her tongue.

"But you admit he has a temper. Maybe it got away from him this time?" I asked.

"I'm done with this conversation." Krissy stormed past me and up the steps.

A gardenia scent floated across the air. The screen door banged shut in her wake.

"That didn't go well," Charlotte said as she walked toward the car.

Minnie was already sitting in the Buick. I stared back at the door. Krissy was nowhere in sight. I turned and headed toward my car. Charlotte got there ahead of me and motioned for me to get in. Glancing over my shoulder, I looked at the front door one last time and realized that my discussion with Krissy hadn't turned out the way that I'd hoped, but I wouldn't let that discourage me. What had I expected? For her to confess? I suppose that would have been great, but not likely.

Chapter 6

Charlotte's Tips for a Fabulous Afterlife

You can say whatever you want.
Most people can't hear you.

When I pulled up in front of my shop, Ken Harrison was leaning on the wall next to the entrance. He'd been looking down staring at his black shiny loafers until he heard my car pull up. Ken was the local attorney who I had befriended. I suppose he wanted to be more than friends, but the timing hadn't been right. Just my luck to meet two fantastic men at the same time.

Ken's appearance was the opposite of Dylan's. Ken had short blond hair and more of a boy-next-door look, while Dylan was a bit more mysterious. They were equally dashingly handsome. Ken wore a gray suit with a crisp white shirt and red tie with blue stripes running diagonal across the fabric. Not vintage, but stylish nonetheless.

I parked the car in front of the shop and got out. The ghosts hurried along beside me. Wind Song had jumped out and was strolling with us too. Charlotte really liked Ken. She had a tough time picking between Ken and Dylan. When Ken was around she liked him better. When Dylan was here she liked him better.

"Who is that?" Minnie asked.

"A handsome man who loves Cookie," Charlotte answered.

"He doesn't love me," I whispered.

Ken didn't know about the ghosts yet. I suppose I should tell him. After all, friends shared things like that, right? Would he still want to be my friend after I told him something crazy like that?

Charlotte looked Ken up and down. "Why so glum, chum?"

Ken had no idea she was talking to him. Or did he sense her? For a second he glanced to his right as if a breeze had lightly touched his face. Charlotte left cool air in her wake everywhere she went. Ken did seem down. Usually the first thing he did when he saw me was offer a smile. He barely mustered a grin this time.

"Ken, I'm surprised to see you here. Is everything okay?" I asked.

"I don't know." He slumped his shoulders. "I guess I just felt like I needed to talk with someone."

"Oh, I hate seeing him like this," Charlotte said.

"He's like a lost puppy dog," Minnie said.

I unlocked the shop door. "Would you like to come inside?"

He ran his hand through his hair. "Sure."

Ken followed me inside, almost unknowingly bumping into Charlotte along the way. Wind Song ran past us and hopped up onto the windowsill to sit in the sunshine. I placed my bag on the counter and faced Ken. He had already taken a seat on the settee.

"He took my seat." Charlotte pointed out.

With a tilt of my head I motioned toward the chair by the dressing room. Charlotte narrowed her eyes and pouted over to the chair.

I sat down next to Ken. "What's wrong? It seems like something is bothering you. You know you can always talk to me."

"You think?" Charlotte called out from the other side of the room. "He's like a chicken with an egg broke in it."

"Look at his big puppy-dog eyes. It's so sad." Minnie stood beside me.

"I'm just trying to adjust to small-town life, I guess. Nothing seems to go according to plans." Ken leaned back on the settee.

"What he means is he wants a girlfriend. Since you show him no love, he is sad." Charlotte had left her chair and joined us.

I knew she wouldn't be able to stay away for long. I hated to admit it, but Charlotte might be on to something. If Ken wanted a girlfriend, that would surely make him down in the dumps. I had no idea how to fix it though. Being around people who were upset made me sad too.

"Maybe you need to take a trip. Go on vacation," I said.

He ran his hand through his hair. "I suppose that is a possibility. Though I have some cases I need to take care of right now."

"You should plan a trip," I said. "As soon as the cases are finished you can take a vacation."

The bell jingled, capturing our attention. We looked over to see who had entered. I'd almost forgotten that it was time for business. This wasn't a customer though. Heather had walked in. She quirked an eyebrow when she saw me sitting on the settee next to Ken. I shrugged. Heather smiled at Minnie and gave a tiny forced grin at Charlotte.

"Well, if it isn't a ray of sunshine coming to greet us this morning," Charlotte said.

Now Heather knew how I felt. She wanted to answer Charlotte, but she couldn't speak to her in front of Ken. Heather would save it up and return the snarkiness to Charlotte later.

"Did I come at a bad time?" Heather asked.

I wasn't sure how much Ken wanted me to say.

"We were just discussing life, I guess," I said.

Heather nodded in understanding. "I know just the thing to help with that."

Ken glanced over at her.

"What's that?" I asked.

"Oh dear. I doubt we want to hear this," Charlotte said.

"What is it, Heather?" Minnie asked.

She was too distracted to answer Minnie.

"I should do a tarot card reading for Ken," Heather said.

He furrowed his brow. "I don't think that's necessary."

"No, I insist. My next appointment isn't for another thirty minutes. That's plenty of time." Heather pulled a deck of cards from her big burlap tote bag. "Come over to the counter and I'll do a reading."

"This should be interesting." Charlotte followed Heather.

"I think this is a bit scary," Minnie said, trailing along behind Charlotte.

Heather had already set up the cards on the counter. I glanced over at Wind Song. Grandma Pearl used the tarot cards to speak to us. Sometimes Wind Song liked to give messages about his favorite food, but most of the time it was Grandma Pearl coming through.

"If you don't want to do this you don't have to," I said.

Ken pushed to his feet. "No, I'll do it. She seems so happy to try. What's the worst that can happen?"

I hoped nothing bad.

Ken and I joined Heather and the ghosts at the counter. Heather had placed the cards facedown on top of the counter. I had a separate set of cards for the cat. On the back of Heather's cards were drawings of beautiful flowers. My cards featured cats in different costumes. It seemed fitting since the cat was the only one who ever used my cards.

Heather looked Ken in the eyes and said, "Pick three cards, but don't turn them over."

Ken studied Heather's face. Next, he reached out and selected three cards.

"Excellent," Heather said.

"I get the feeling that Ken doesn't believe in all this hocus-pocus," Charlotte said.

Charlotte might be surprised. Something told me there was a lot about Ken that we didn't know. He might seem like the boy next door, but he also seemed quite passionate, and of course he was extremely intelligent.

Heather picked up the three cards and turned them over.

She tapped the first card, which featured a woman in a long white gown. "Someone new is about to come into your life."

Charlotte and I exchanged a look. Wow. It was as if Heather knew what we'd been talking about. Maybe her gift was much better than we realized.

She studied the next card, which had two women standing side by side with sunlight behind them. "You shouldn't look to the past."

Ken had seemed guarded at first with his arms crossed in front of his chest. Now he'd relaxed his arms to his side.

Heather checked the last card, which depicted three small children in a garden. "Open your eyes to what's in front of you."

Ken's eyes widened as he stared at Heather.

Heather gathered up the cards. "Wow, you know,

I'm not sure where all that came from. I usually don't read cards with that much intensity. The energy in here is thick."

Minnie stood behind Heather. I wasn't sure why she was smiling, but she seemed happy with Heather's reading.

"I think you did a great job, Heather," Ken said. "You're fantastic."

Charlotte and I exchanged smiles. Heather blushed at the compliment.

"Yeah, well, thanks." She stuffed the cards into her bag. "I guess I should be going. I don't want to be late for my appointment."

"Thanks, Heather," I said.

"I'll call you later." Heather rushed toward the door.

"Bye," Ken called out in Heather's wake.

"That was weird," Charlotte said.

"I should be going too." Ken gestured over his shoulder. "Thanks for talking to me, Cookie."

I reached out and wrapped my arms around Ken. "You know you can talk to me anytime."

He stared me in the eyes. "I'm glad I have a friend like you, Cookie."

"Oh stop; you're going to make me cry," Charlotte said, wiping at her eyes.

"I'm already crying," Minnie said with a sniffle.

I released my hold on Ken. "Okay, I should let you go now."

He touched my chin with his index finger. "I'll see you soon."

We watched as Ken walked out the door. I'd felt the energy Heather had talked about. However, the sensation had faded now that Heather and Ken had gone. It was strange, but I had no explanation for it.

"Such a nice man," Charlotte said dreamily.

"If only we could play matchmaker," Minnie said. "Who could you set him up with?"

"Oh no, I'm not doing that. It would only cause problems." I grabbed a hanger for a blouse. "We'll just mind our own business."

"Since when do we mind our own business? Problems for who? Ken or you?" Charlotte asked.

"For Ken, of course," I said.

Minnie and Charlotte looked at each other.

"If you say so," Charlotte said with a click of her tongue.

Chapter 7

Cookie's Savvy Tips for Vintage Shopping

*If you're looking for a one-of-a-kind gift,
give vintage clothing a try.
The recipient might love a unique piece of jewelry
or a stunning scarf from bygone days.*

I flipped the sign on the door. It was late when I finally closed the shop for the evening. Not long ago I'd hired a part-time employee, but she only worked about ten hours a week. I hoped to have Brianna work more when business picked up.

I'd planned on making dinner at home, but now I was too hungry. That meant there was only one thing to do. I decided to stop by Glorious Grits for a quick bite. It was time I paid a visit to Dixie Bryant anyway. The walk from my shop to the diner was a short one, so I left the car parked out front and headed across the street. Wind Song always stayed at the shop while I grabbed a quick bite. Dixie should change her policy about having cats in her diner. Especially since it had been Grandma Pearl's favorite restaurant.

Of course Charlotte and Minnie were with me as

I walked down the sidewalk toward the diner. When a newly acquired ghost arrived in my life, they usually stuck around me like used glue from an old sticker. At least that had been my experience, but maybe it was different for others. Charlotte knew the ins and outs of the ghost world now though, so she had a tendency to pop back and forth between worlds. Charlotte had a beau on the other side, and she was torn between hanging out with her best living friend and her best dearly departed friend. She'd tried to explain all of this to me, but it was a bit difficult to understand. Most of the time I just smiled while she talked.

"Cookie, I've warned you repeatedly about the calorie content at Glorious Grits. Or should I call it Un-glorious Grits," Charlotte said as she walked beside me.

"And I told you I'm having a salad, not an entire cherry pie." I held my phone up to my ear so that people wouldn't think I was talking to myself.

"Make sure to get the low-fat dressing," Charlotte warned.

"What's low-fat dressing?" Minnie asked.

"You know, without the fat," Charlotte said. "I'm just trying to keep her healthy, that's all."

"I'm so glad you all can discuss my eating habits as if I'm not even here," I said.

"Any time," Charlotte said with a smirk.

When I reached the door, I opened it and walked inside the diner. A country song I didn't recognize played on the radio. Oldies was usually the only thing that ever played on my radio, so I wasn't aware of any new hits. The smell of burgers and fries drifted through the air. My mouth watered, but I had to remember Charlotte's words. If she could she'd knock the food out of my hand. The diner was filled with eclectic décor. Various types of art decorated the walls, and red and white table-cloths covered the tables. Dixie was behind the counter ringing up someone's ticket. She glanced up and a huge smile spread across her face.

"Cookie, I'm surprised to see you." She handed the customer change and stepped out from behind the counter. "What brings you by?"

She wore jeans, a white T-shirt, and the red and white polka-dot apron. Dixie was petite with short blond hair. She always bounced around the diner like she was on a trampoline.

"I worked late tonight so I decided to stop by for dinner." I sat on one of the stools at the counter.

"Did you find a lot of gorgeous clothes today?" she asked.

"Yeah, something like that," I said with a little less enthusiasm than I normally displayed.

"Are you dining in tonight?"

"No, I should get home. I'll take it to go."

"What will you have?" she asked with a smile.

"The usual," I said.

Dixie watched me as she poured a Diet Coke for me. "What happened in the cemetery was terrible. I'm so sorry."

"Thank you," I said, taking the drink from her.

She looked around me. "Did a ghost show up?"

I'd told Dixie about the ghosts. I knew she believed me and wouldn't think I was crazy.

Diners were sitting at the booths nearby, but none close enough to hear our conversation. At least I hoped they couldn't hear.

"Actually, a ghost did pop up," I said.

Her eyes widened. "Oh, the photographer?"

"No, her name is Minnie Lynn." I glanced over at Minnie.

She was looking around the diner and heard me mention her name.

"Who is she?" Dixie asked.

"I'm not sure. She says she's from the 1920s. So far that's all the info I have."

I needed to find out more about her. Of course that would have to be added to my to-do list. Maybe tomorrow I could stop by the library or speak with the town historian.

"Oh wow. That's interesting, Cookie. How will you find out what she wants?"

"Find out what who wants?" Minnie had returned her attention to me again.

"They were discussing finding out why you're here. What made you pop up all of a sudden?" Charlotte said.

Minnie's eyes widened. "Yes, I would love that. Definitely I want Cookie to do that. Only when she has the extra time though. No hurry. We have all the time in the world."

Minnie winked at me.

"Sorry, the ghosts were talking. What did you say, Dixie?"

"I was asking how you will find out what the new ghost wants," Dixie said, looking around as if she'd spot the ghosts.

"That's a good question. She doesn't know. I guess that leaves me with tracking down the info."

"I don't know anyone who would have information like that." Dixie pulled my order from the back service window. "Oh, wait, you should speak with the town historian. She might have info on that name." Dixie placed my salad in a brown paper bag with the diner's logo on the front.

"Yes, I was just thinking about that. It's a good idea. Thank you, Dixie." I took the paper bag with my dinner.

"This is exciting, but remember you have to solve the murder case first," Minnie said.

"Don't you want her to find out about you?" Charlotte asked.

Minnie waved her hand. "Oh, there's plenty of time."

"So what's she like?" Dixie whispered.

Minnie stood closer to my side now. She watched Dixie with her wide big blue eyes.

"She's a sweetie," I said. "A charming personality. As long as she doesn't pick up Charlotte's bad habits."

"Hey, I'm right here." Charlotte scowled.

"Thank you, Cookie," Minnie said.

Dixie looked around. "How's Charlotte doing with this?"

Charlotte placed her hands on her hips. "Charlotte is just fine."

"They get along well," I said.

"Of course we do. I get along with everyone," Charlotte said.

"Well, that's good news," Dixie said, still searching for the ghosts.

Minnie gestured. "Cookie, aren't they the men you talked to at the hotel? They told you about Darrin."

"It is them, Cookie. You should sit in the booth next to them. Maybe you'll overhear more talk about Darrin," Charlotte said.

"Don't you think they will recognize me and stop talking?" I asked.

"Well, it's worth a shot," Charlotte said. "What have you got to lose?"

"Nothing, I guess," I said around a sigh. "Okay, Dixie, I want to get this for here."

"Sure thing," Dixie said. "I'll get you a plate and silverware."

"Just the fork and a napkin is fine," I said.

"Eating out of a Styrofoam container?" Charlotte asked with a shake of her head. "What's next? Eating right off the table with your face down in it?"

"Oh stop, Charlotte, this is no time for one of your fancy dinner parties."

I walked over to the booth beside the men, trying

to act nonchalant. So far they hadn't looked up. Sliding into the booth, I listened to their conversation. They were talking about cars and weightlifting.

"This is boring talk. I wish we could guide their conversation," Charlotte said.

"Maybe we can," Minnie said.

"How can we do that?" I whispered.

"Maybe if they saw something that reminded them of the topic," Minnie said.

"No offense, honey, but I don't think that's possible." Charlotte gave Minnie a pitying look.

"Did you hear Krissy talking about the murder?" the guy asked.

My eyes widened. I leaned back so I could hear every word. I hoped they didn't notice my actions. If they knew I was listening they'd stop talking.

"What did she say?" the other guy asked. "Do you think she did it?"

"I don't know. It's possible. She claimed she thought it was Tyler's ex-girlfriend."

There was a pause in the conversation.

"What are they doing?" I whispered.

"Stuffing their faces with french fries," Charlotte said.

"I hope they go back to the conversation," I said.

"I hope so too. They can't leave us hanging like that." Charlotte stared over my shoulder at the men.

"Who is the ex-girlfriend?" the guy asked.

Thank goodness they went back to the talk.

"Her name is Tina Fairchild. From what I heard she is a bit crazy."

Another pause in the conversation.

"He stuffed a french fry in his mouth," Charlotte said.

"She didn't want to break up," he added.

"Crazy ex-girlfriend. That would make sense." Charlotte lifted an eyebrow. "There's only one problem with that. We didn't see her anywhere at the scene."

"Could she have snuck around the back and left the cemetery some way?" Minnie asked.

"There's a fence all around the place," I said.

"Yes, but it's not a tall fence so she could have jumped over," Charlotte said.

"That's true. I suppose she could have done that." I lifted my fork and took a bite.

I'd almost forgotten to eat.

"Did you say something?" the man asked.

I froze with my fork in midair.

"They're looking over at you," Charlotte whispered, as if they could hear her.

When I looked over my shoulder, I realized he was talking to me. Both men were staring at me.

"Oh, we meet again," I said, trying to act casual.

He frowned. "Were you listening to our conversation?"

"This won't end well. He looks angry," Charlotte said.

"I'd say the other one is upset too based on his pinched eyebrows." Minnie pointed.

"Um, well, I couldn't exactly not hear. You were talking kind of loud." I attempted a smile.

The men stared at me. Apparently my smile wasn't working. The other one had turned around in the booth to get a good look.

When they didn't speak, I continued the conversation. "Since you brought up the subject though. Could you tell me about this Tina Fairchild?"

One of them laughed. "What are you, a private detective?"

The other one laughed. "Yeah, she's a real Nancy Drew."

Now they were making me mad.

"This guy is a jerk," Charlotte said.

Charlotte's eyebrows furrowed. She tried never to scowl. The fact that she was now doing it meant she was extremely angry. I'd better get her out of here before she did something to these guys. Like knock their Cokes into their laps.

"I'm not a private eye, but I do care about murder in my town," I snapped.

"You tell him, Cookie," Minnie said.

Charlotte stood from the booth and walked over to their table. She crossed her arms in front of her chest, stared at them, and tapped her foot against the tile floor.

The guy closest to me stared for a beat and asked, "What do you want to know?"

"Tyler was having problems with an ex-girlfriend?" I asked.

He set his fork down. "Yeah, but we never saw her."

"How do you know she was doing anything?" I asked.

"Our girlfriends told us. Tyler told them all about it," he said.

"What kind of crazy things was she doing?" I pressed.

"How Tina didn't want to break up and wouldn't take no for an answer," the guy farthest from me said.

"That's not much help. Looks like you'd be better off talking with the models," Charlotte said.

"What else can you tell me?"

The guy behind me shrugged. "That's all I know."

"Thanks," I said, feeling a bit defeated.

The men stood from the booth. "Nice seeing you again."

I knew by the smirk on his face that he wasn't sincere. It didn't matter though. I had to find Tina Fairchild and ask her some questions.

Chapter 8

Charlotte's Tips for a Fabulous Afterlife

―――――――

Talk the living into doing things
they might not normally do.
It's fun to watch their reaction.

"Why did I let you talk me into this?" I asked as I shone the flashlight around the darkened graveyard.

"Hey, if you walk by a graveyard with an unlocked gate I consider that an invitation." Charlotte trailed along behind me.

Easy for her to say. She was using me as a shield. Plus, she was a ghost. If anything happened I'd be the one to deal with it. Minnie was on my other side. She was trying to hold on to my arm as if that offered protection. All I felt was the cold air from her touch. If it made her feel better though I was fine with that.

After finishing the salad, I'd been on my way home when we drove past the graveyard. Charlotte had spotted the open gate and insisted that I turn around. Parking the Buick down the street a bit so that no one would notice it in front of the grave-yard, I walked over and entered the cemetery with my knees practically knocking. I jumped at every rustle of a branch and hoot of an owl. Charlotte pretended to be brave, but she was no less scared than me. Though she'd never admit it.

All I had to guide me around the headstones was the tiny light emanating from my phone. I pointed it toward the ground so that I wouldn't step on something and trip. I hoped not another dead body.

"Why exactly am I here?" I asked. "It's not as if the police forgot something. Dylan is extremely thorough in his investigations."

"I'm not trying to insult Dylan. Bless his heart, I know he's good, but he's only human, which means he could have missed something," Charlotte said.

Holding the phone to my face so that the flashlight would highlight my expression for her, I gave her a warning stare. She'd added the "bless his heart" part so it wouldn't seem like an insult. I knew her tricks.

"Well, there's no way I would ever tell him that. Plus, what if he finds out I was here? He'll think I have no faith in him."

A rustling noise came from my right and I spun the light around.

"There's nothing there. You're just being paranoid," Charlotte said.

"Let's just look around so I can get out of here," I said.

"That's what I've been wanting to do if you'd stop chattering." Charlotte stepped in front of me.

"It's eerie in here. As if someone is watching us."

Minnie rubbed her arms as if she was fighting off a chill.

The air was warm still, but a cool breeze had blown past. When I came to the area where I'd discovered Tyler's body, I froze. A chill traveled down my spine. It was even scarier in the dark of night.

"What if there are bad ghosts out here?" I whispered.

"Don't worry, Cookie, ghosts can't kill you. If they could Heather might be gone by now." Charlotte chuckled.

"Charlotte! That's not very nice," I scolded.

She held her hands up. "I'm kidding."

I quirked an eyebrow. With Charlotte I could never be sure.

"Maybe there was some kind of significance to the grave where Tyler was found," Minnie said.

She wasn't getting involved with the bickering between Charlotte and me. That was probably a good decision.

"That could be true." I stepped closer to the gravestone and shone the light on it. "But what is it?"

The stone marker was tall and skinny. A simple cross was etched at the top with the name GILBERT MCNALLEY below. The birthdate and date of death were listed underneath that: MARCH 19, 1845 TO AUGUST 23, 1922.

"He was seventy-seven years old when he died," I said.

"Good math," Charlotte quipped.

"This still gives me no clues." I moved the light around the grave. I had no idea what else I thought I might find.

"Perhaps you should research the name," Minnie suggested.

"Yes, I suppose that's a good place to start." I shifted the light behind me and turned around. "What's that?"

"What's what?" Charlotte asked.

"There's something shiny way over there under the tree." My light was reflecting off the object.

We headed over toward the gnarly oak tree. I weaved around the gravestones and stopped next to the trunk. On the ground was a phone.

"What is it?" Minnie asked as she clung to my side.

I reached down and picked it up. "Someone lost their phone."

"Maybe it's the killer's," Charlotte said.

I swiped the screen and it lit up. "It hasn't been here long or it wouldn't still be charged."

"Who does it belong to? The suspense is killing me," Minnie said. "Can you see a name on that device? Who knew that telephones would be portable and hid in a pocket?"

Charlotte laughed.

After examining the phone, I looked at Charlotte. "The phone belonged to Tyler."

Minnie gasped.

"You're kidding me," Charlotte said.

"How did the police miss this?" I asked.

Charlotte gave me a sideways glance.

"Don't even say that Dylan isn't good at his job," I warned.

Charlotte held her hand up in surrender. "Of course not. Someone else missed it."

"What information can you find from it?" Minnie asked.

I scrolled through to the text messages. "There's a text from a woman named Shanna. This would have been right before Tyler's death."

"That doesn't mean it has anything to do with the text, right?" Charlotte asked.

"No, but we need to find this woman. Maybe she knows something about why Tyler would have been killed."

"Do you have a last name? How will you find her?" Charlotte asked.

"The name is Shanna Sizemore. Considering her phone number is here, I think I have a good chance of finding her," I said.

Charlotte gestured. "Good point."

"What are you waiting for? Go find her." Minnie motioned for me to move.

"It's late. We'll have to wait until tomorrow," I said.

Minnie released an audible breath.

"What will you do with the phone?" Charlotte asked.

"I suppose I need to give the phone to Dylan." I turned the phone over in my hand.

Charlotte raised an eyebrow. "Right, but not

before getting all the information you need from it."

"That's not right. I shouldn't do that, but I will," I said.

"I knew you would," Charlotte said with a smile.

Leaves rustled and something jumped down at us from one of the gnarly branches. I screamed and fell backward, landing on the ground. Thank goodness I hadn't been near the graves. A streak of black zipped across my path and disappeared around a headstone.

"Cookie, this is no time for relaxing." Charlotte wiggled her finger in my direction.

I quirked an eyebrow at Charlotte.

"What was that?" Minnie asked, clutching her chest. "Cookie, are you all right?"

I was still trying to catch my breath, but I managed to push to my feet.

"Thank goodness it was just a cat," I said.

"Where did it come from? I think it was trying to attack us." Charlotte scanned the area, looking for the cat.

"It jumped from the tree. The cat was probably just scared," I said.

Speaking of cats, Grandma Pearl was waiting for us in the car. I needed to hurry back before she got angry. She'd refused to come into the graveyard with us. I pointed the phone toward the ground, allowing the sliver of light to slice through the dark and guide the way. Though it was hard to see, I tried to hurry back out of the graveyard. I was grateful to leave my spooky surroundings.

Once out of the cemetery's gate, I paused.

"What are you doing?" Charlotte had rushed right through me. "I hate when you stop in front of me and I travel through you. It's like I've just been through an amusement park with cotton candy and rainbows."

The cat from the tree was now sitting on the hood of my car. He was staring into the car at Wind Song. Charlotte and Minnie followed me, spotting the mysterious feline.

"Don't scare my grandmother," I said, rushing over to the Buick.

I'd expected the cat to race away once it saw me. However, he remained on the hood, watching Wind Song through the windshield. Wind Song hissed. I wasn't sure if it was the cat or my grandmother doing that. Knowing Grandma Pearl, if she decided she didn't like this stranger, it was probably her giving that reaction.

"Good kitty," I said as I approached.

"I hope he doesn't attack you," Charlotte said. "Just tell the thing to get lost."

I eased closer to the car, hoping the cat would jump off the hood. The cat turned to face me and hissed at me.

"Well, he's a friendly one," Charlotte said.

"Maybe we should back away until he leaves," Minnie said.

Charlotte pointed. "No way. He's not the boss."

"What will I do with him?" I asked. "He won't let me get near, I'm sure. From the looks of his behavior he won't allow me to pick him up either."

"I've never seen a cat that stubborn," Charlotte.

"He reminds me of you, Charlotte," Minnie said.

Charlotte put her hands on her hips and glared at Minnie.

"Come on, kitty, I have to go now. Shouldn't you go home too?" I asked in the sweetest voice possible.

"He's not going to answer you," Charlotte said.

I raised an eyebrow. "Or will he?"

"You don't think . . . ?" Charlotte asked.

"No, it can't be," I said with a wave of my hand.

"Can't be what?" Minnie asked.

"Well, he could be. After all, look at your grandmother." Charlotte motioned.

Grandma Pearl was focused on the cat. He was now licking his paws as he remained on the hood.

"He's doing this on purpose," I said.

"Why would he do that?" Charlotte asked.

"Oh, now I get it. Maybe if you talk to him like you do Wind Song," Minnie said.

"Kitty, is there something wrong?" I asked.

He stopped licking his paw and meowed. His stare was focused on me.

"I think that means yes," Charlotte said.

"He doesn't appear sick. What's wrong, kitty?" I asked.

If anyone heard me talking to ghosts and a cat, they'd think I'd lost my marbles.

The cat stayed on the car hood and ventured closer to the open window of my car, toward my grandmother. Grandma Pearl stopped her verbal warning and stared at him. She must be in shock as much as we were.

"I guess he wants a ride," Charlotte said.

"He might just be lost and scared. I'll have to try to find his home," I said.

The Ouija board was still on my mind. I suppose if I just happened to have the board out and the cat decided to use it . . . No, that was a crazy thought. What were the odds that it would happen again? Though I suppose if it was possible once, it could happen again.

"That's good that you want to help him, but how will you get him in the car?" Charlotte asked.

"Maybe you could catch him with something," Minnie said.

Charlotte snorted. "If she wants to put her life in her own hands, I guess she could try it."

I inched toward the car. Any sudden move and he could jump and attack me. Although he might run away. I hated to let him get away if he needed help. Someone could be searching for him right now. With his bright yellow eyes he watched my every move. I couldn't tell if he planned to allow me to put him in the car or if he wanted to attack once I was close enough. I held my breath and reached out for the car door. Thank goodness he hadn't moved an inch. I opened the door as he watched me.

"Now what will you do?" Charlotte asked.

"I don't have that much planned out yet," I said.

The cat pushed to all fours, meowed, and jumped down from the hood. Thank goodness he wasn't acting as if he wanted to scratch me. He moved around the door and in one leap was inside the car. He sat on the seat next to Grandma Pearl.

"I can't believe it," Charlotte said.

"I think he wants a ride," Minnie said.

Wind Song or Grandma Pearl, whichever was there at the moment, was staring at the cat, but luckily they were getting along.

"Well, I guess we should get out of here." I closed the door and hurried over to the driver's side.

The cats meowed loudly when Charlotte tried to sit on them. She wouldn't give up her seat in the front of the car for anyone. With the cats next to me in the middle of the seat, Charlotte on the passenger side, and Minnie in the backseat, I pulled away from the curb and headed home.

Chapter 9

Cookie's Savvy Tips for Vintage Shopping

*Coats and jackets are another great way
to incorporate vintage clothing into your life.
They add just the right amount of vintage style.*

I'd brought the cat home with me. He'd refused to eat any of the cat food I had for Wind Song, though he had devoured the tuna I offered and a saucer of milk. I'd have to make a trip to the Piggly Wiggly today and pick up a different kind of food for him. There had to be some flavor he liked. I knew Wind Song would be happy she wouldn't have to share her food. My grandmother didn't care. She was just stuck in the cat's body, so she tolerated the seafood fare. However, Grandma Pearl refused to allow Wind Song to chase mice or any other rodents.

I'd wanted to use the Ouija board or tarot cards last night. Not that I was totally convinced this cat would say anything. Actually, I was pretty sure he wouldn't, but curiosity was getting the better of me. Curiosity killed the cat, right? Okay, bad pun, but anyway, I just hoped that saying wasn't true this time. Besides, the board and cards were back at the shop. It had been a long day and I'd wanted to get home and look at Tyler's phone. I'd unearthed more information by searching through it. His ex-girlfriend had been harassing him. She'd made no direct threats, but her persistence was unnerving.

The messages had started less threatening with her writing things like: *How can I live without you? Please don't leave me.* They'd escalated to things like: *You won't get away with this. You'll be sorry for what you've done to me.*

The discovery of the phone definitely sent the ex-girlfriend to the top of my suspect list. I was glad that I'd found Tyler's phone in the graveyard and that I'd seen the messages. Would I be able to contact her? She probably wouldn't answer my questions.

I'd called Dylan this morning and told him I had something for him. It wouldn't be fun explaining exactly how I'd found it. Though it was almost as if it was meant for me to locate the phone. The gate had been open when it normally wouldn't have been. It was practically like an invitation. Though I doubted Dylan would see it that way. Plus the cat had obviously made the sound, which had alerted me in the direction of the phone. Had he done that on purpose? As soon as I spoke with Dylan and gave him the phone, I'd pull out the Ouija board and see if the cat wanted to chat.

Right now I was in the Buick and headed toward my shop. Once again Charlotte was beside me with Minnie in the back. Grandma Pearl and the new cat were sitting in the backseat as well. They were actually getting along quite nicely now. I wish I knew what this cat's name was. Once the veterinarian's office opened, I'd give them a call so I could bring the cat in and have them scan for owner information.

Even though I'd been in a hurry this morning, I still took the time to pick out the best outfit I could find for today. Charlotte had suggested evening wear, but I'd told her that was a bit much for this time of day. I'd gone with a pale yellow Gucci dress that buttoned all the way down the front. My shoes were brown heels and my bag matched. The day always felt better when I dressed in vintage from head to toe.

I pulled the Buick up to the curb in front of the shop and cut the engine. "Well, everyone, looks like we've got a busy day ahead of us."

"Vintage clothing, check. Communicating with cats via Ouija board, check. Tracking down a murderer, check." Charlotte ticked each one off with her fingers.

"All in a day's work for Cookie," Minnie said.

I got out of the car and moved around to the back door. Grandma Pearl knew the routine. I opened the door and she graciously leaped to the sidewalk like a ballerina. She strolled over to the shop's door to wait for me to open it. Since he showed no signs of moving, I reached in the car to grab the new cat. He wouldn't know the routine, and he was probably still scared. However, he wasn't having any of my holding him. He wiggled until he was able to jump from my arms. Once on the sidewalk, he rushed over and stood beside Grandma Pearl.

"He knows exactly what he's doing," Charlotte said. "If I didn't know better I'd say he's been here before."

To my shock, it appeared that the cat really was aware of what he was doing. Was Grandma Pearl able to communicate with him? This grew crazier by the minute. If I hadn't seen it with my own eyes I wouldn't believe it. Had he been here before?

Once the door was open and unlocked the cats rushed inside. Wind Song was in charge this morning because she took the spot in the window to get sunshine. I suppose Grandma Pearl would talk with us later. I hoped she didn't wait too long though, because I wanted to hear her opinion on the new cat.

Everyone hurried inside in front of me. They spread out like I'd dropped marbles on the floor. Charlotte went to the settee. Minnie was at the counter waiting for me. Wind Song was at her favorite spot in the window, and the black cat took the other side. He stared out the window as if he were waiting for someone. I went through my normal routine of opening the shop. The mannequins in the front window needed to be changed, but I'd have to do that later. Recently, I'd found a rare Pierre Cardin gem. It was a shift dress in a stunning shade of turquoise. The piece was more than clothing. It was a work of art and deserved to be displayed as such.

I'd just started sorting through a few new items when Dylan walked through the door. He wore gray slacks with pleats in the front and a light blue Armani button-down shirt.

"He's looking handsome as usual," Charlotte said. "So easy on the eyes."

"He is a swell guy," Minnie said around a sigh.

"I like the way his muscles are so proportionate." Charlotte soaked in Dylan's appearance from head to toe.

"I like the way his full lips form a perfect pout. And don't get me started on that thick head of dark hair." Minnie twisted the pearl necklace around her neck with her index finger as she eyed Dylan.

"Meeooww," Grandma Pearl said.

What would Dylan say if he knew about Charlotte's and Minnie's comments? He would probably blush. He might have a tough detective demeanor, but for some things he was still a bit shy.

He smiled. "Good morning, gorgeous."

My cheeks flushed. "Good morning."

Minnie placed her cheeks into her hands as she propped her elbows on the counter. She stared at us. "Oh, look at the lovebirds. It's a match made in heaven."

"Mushy and sickening, isn't it?" Charlotte said.

"I think it's sweet," Minnie said.

The new cat jumped up onto the counter and meowed loudly at Dylan.

"Well, who's this?" Dylan asked, reaching out toward the cat.

When the cat hissed he quickly moved his hand away. I supposed now was as good a time as any to tell him what I'd done last night.

"The cat kind of found me," I said.

Dylan chuckled. "Funny how they find you, isn't it? Did he stroll into the shop like Wind Song?"

I still needed to tell Dylan about Grandma Pearl. How did you tell someone that your dead grandmother was now taking over a cat's body? It might be easy to speak the words, but once they were out there I'd be under a twenty-four-hour psychiatric hold.

I laughed nervously. "Yes, that is strange how they find me. He didn't walk into the shop though."

"So where did you find him?" Dylan quirked an eyebrow.

He had obviously picked up on my uneasiness.

"You know how Charlotte always has weird ideas?" I asked.

"Hey, don't pin this on me." Charlotte pointed.

"Well, it was technically your idea," Minnie said.

Charlotte glared at Minnie, but Minnie didn't care. Minnie had this adorable naïveté about her. I doubted Minnie even picked up on Charlotte's crankiness.

Dylan studied my face. "Yes, I suppose."

"Well, she had another weird one last night," I said. "You'll really like this one."

His expression turned to a slight frown. "What's that?"

"No matter how sweet you try to act, he's not going to like this," Charlotte said.

Charlotte wasn't helping matters. I just needed to say it. Dylan would have to get over it. What was done was done.

"Well, I was passing by the graveyard and Charlotte suggested that I have a look around." I straightened the bracelets on the display so that I wouldn't have to look at him.

"Do you always do what Charlotte tells you to do?" Dylan asked.

"Yes, she does." Charlotte studied her perfectly painted red fingernails. "It serves her well to listen to me. I know what I'm talking about."

"No, I don't always do what she says, but I suppose it didn't seem like a horrible idea. And now I'm glad that I followed through with it."

"Why is that?" Dylan crossed his arms in front of his chest.

I reached under the counter and pulled out my purse. The phone was in the plastic bag. I handed it to him. "I found Tyler's phone last night in the graveyard."

He looked at the phone and back to me.

I held the bag up. "It's true. I looked at it to see who it belonged to. So my fingerprints will be on it."

"Your fingerprints are on a lot of things," he said, taking the bag from my outstretched hand.

"Oh, he doesn't sound happy with you," Minnie said. "This match made in heaven might be in jeopardy."

"Better call Ken. He might need to bail you out," Charlotte said. "Cookie, you can't wear vintage in prison."

"Where did you find it in the graveyard? We searched everywhere," Dylan said.

"It was underneath a tree. Maybe the killer came back and dropped it?" I suggested. "You know they sometimes take something from the victim as a memento."

I didn't want him to think that they had missed such an important clue.

"Yes, I'm aware. I think it's unlikely the killer returned," he said.

Charlotte shook her head. "Honestly, Cookie, the things you come up with. Why would the killer do something like that?"

Maybe a ghost had harassed the killer into doing it.

"I suppose I don't need to look at the phone to find out what's on it. You can tell me? Since you decided to wait until today to tell me about it. You could have called last night."

Charlotte laughed. "He's even cuter when he's angry."

"This is an awkward conversation," Minnie said.

Yes, it was awkward, but I didn't regret going into

the graveyard and finding the phone. I didn't even regret looking at it. I would stand my ground.

"I think he had an ex-girlfriend who may have been stalking him. Plus, there's another woman that he was speaking with that I would like to talk with." I gestured toward the phone.

"I bet you would," Dylan said. "Would you also like the police department to hire you?"

"Only if they have vintage uniforms," Charlotte said around a laugh.

"Oh, you stay out of it," I snapped.

I hadn't meant to talk with Charlotte while Dylan was around. Even though he was aware of her, it was still awkward. Dylan's eyes widened and he looked in the direction where I'd shot a glare at Charlotte.

"Problems with the ghosts?" Dylan asked.

"Charlotte's being a bit testy." I narrowed my eyes at her.

"Oh," he said, glancing to his left.

"Over here." Charlotte waved from his right.

"Where does the new cat fit into all this?" Dylan asked.

The cat meowed, as if he knew what Dylan had said. We stared at him and he stared back.

"He was in the graveyard. When he made a noise it drew my attention to the area where I found the phone. It was almost as if he was trying to show me the phone," I said.

Dylan chuckled. "That's impossible."

We stared at the cat again. Was it impossible?

Dylan held up the bag. "Okay, I'll look into this, but in the meantime, no snooping around, please?"

No snooping around? Was Dylan serious? There was no way I could agree to that.

"I'll stay out of trouble," I said with a smile.

"See how she does that?" Charlotte asked Minnie. "She didn't agree to no snooping. She just said she'd stay out of trouble. Now he assumes that she means no snooping. I've taught her well."

Minnie's shoulders slumped slightly. "It's hard to keep her out of trouble."

Chapter 10

Charlotte's Tips for a Fabulous Afterlife

———

Never claim to be an expert with the paranormal.
It will only get you in trouble.

Now that Dylan had gone it was time for me to ask this cat a few questions. The mystery cat had acted . . . well, mysterious. Now I couldn't stop wondering if he had led me to the phone on purpose. I pulled out the Ouija board from under the counter and placed it on top.

Grandma Pearl jumped down from the window and headed over to the counter. Usually that meant she wanted to communicate by using the board, but this time I wasn't sure. Maybe she just wanted to hear what this cat had to say.

"Come here, kitty. Do you want to use the board?" I gestured with my index finger.

"Oh, for heaven's sake, I've seen it all now." Charlotte shook her head.

"What do you mean you've seen it all? If Grandma Pearl can use the board, then this cat might too. He obviously knows what's going on around here."

Charlotte snorted. "If you say so."

"I think Cookie's right. The cat wants us to know something." Minnie waved at the cat.

"Thank you, Minnie," I said.

As Grandma Pearl strolled past the black cat she looked over at him. He got up and walked with her. They jumped up on the counter.

I smirked. "See, I told you he knows what's going on around here. Grandma Pearl must be talking to him."

Charlotte tossed her hands up. "Fine. Maybe he does. Let's see what this cat has to say."

"I can't wait to see what the cat has to say." Minnie practically bounced as she paced across the room.

Wind Song jumped up on the counter and the black cat followed. I had assumed Grandma Pearl was in charge of the cat's body. Maybe I was wrong. What if Wind Song just wanted to request more tuna treats? The cats sat side by side, peering down at the board. After a few seconds of Grandma Pearl staring at the board, she shifted her gaze to the cat, as if to say *Well, what are you waiting for?*

We waited with bated breath for something to happen. After a couple more seconds passed, the cat reached out and placed its paw on the planchette. I didn't dare move a muscle, because I didn't want to scare the cat from proceeding. The cat moved the planchette around the board just like Grandma Pearl did when she used it.

"What is your name?" I asked.

The planchette whirled around the board with the push of the cat's paw. Finally he stopped on the letter *T*. He licked his paws again.

"Looks like he is just goofing off," Charlotte said.

"This is no time to play games, kitty," I said.

I thought Charlotte was right until the cat placed his paw on the planchette again.

"Look, he's starting again." Minnie pointed.

He pushed the thing around before slowing down and stopping on the letter *Y*.

"*T Y*? Are those his initials?" Minnie asked.

Charlotte and I exchanged a look. When the cat continued to the letter *L*, I knew the answer.

"*Tyler.*" The name slipped from my lips almost as a whisper.

I couldn't believe what was happening. How had this happened?

"For once I'm speechless," Charlotte said.

"And that never happens," Minnie said.

"It can't be, right?" I looked at Charlotte.

Tyler stared at me as if to say *Believe it*.

"Tyler is the man who was murdered in the graveyard?" Minnie asked in shock.

"The one and only," Charlotte said with a click of her tongue.

"How did that happen?" Minnie asked.

"I don't know. There had been a séance when my grandmother got into the cat's body. There certainly wasn't a séance the day that Tyler was murdered," I said.

"That we know of," Charlotte said.

"Everyone was taking photos, not calling to the dead."

"You know, I can't believe I'm going to say this." Charlotte released a big sigh. "You should ask Heather about this. She has all those books on the paranormal. Maybe she has the answer." Charlotte shivered. "Can't believe I said that."

Was Charlotte softening up to Heather? I thought she'd always secretly liked Heather's strength and independence.

"That's a good idea," I said. "In the meantime, I have work around here. I'll tell her we'll stop by after work. Is there anything else you'd like to say . . . Tyler?"

Yes, it felt strange calling the cat by name. Could it be a coincidence? That was unlikely. I shouldn't be too surprised that Tyler was in a cat's body. It had happened to Grandma Pearl, so it could happen to Tyler too. Apparently Tyler had more to say because he moved that planchette again.

"I hope he's not going to tell you what kind of food to buy," Charlotte said.

I kept track of the letters as he slid the pointer around the board. He stopped on *G* first, moving on to the *E*.

"Get?" I said.

The cat continued. After a few more letters he stopped and I had a full sentence.

"*Get me out of here*," I repeated the words.

Charlotte laughed. "Now that's funny."

I stared at Tyler. "Can you tell me how you got in there?"

Tyler looked away. I suppose that was a no. Now I had to find out how this had happened.

"I know you want out of the cat's body, Tyler, but there's an important question I need answered right now," I said. "Who killed you?"

"Oh yes, that is something he can tell us," Minnie said excitedly.

With any luck he would share that information.

"Okay, Tyler, tell us what you know," Charlotte said.

To my relief, Tyler moved the planchette again. He was surprisingly good at this, considering he'd only been a cat for a short time. I followed his paw as he glided over the letters. He'd spelled out three sentences this time. He was good at this, but not giving the information we needed to solve this crime.

"*I don't know. Get me out of here. It smells like fish,*" I repeated his message.

My eyes widened.

"How can you not know who killed you?" Charlotte placed her hands on her hips.

"You didn't know," I reminded her.

"Oh right," she said through pursed lips.

Tyler may have finished using the board, but when Grandma Pearl placed her paw on the planchette, I knew she had something to say.

"What is it, Grandma?" I asked.

She moved the pointer around the board and spelled out a few words.

Tyler wants out of there.

"Well, I can understand that he does, and will try to help him, but it takes time."

"He's even pushy when he's a cat," Charlotte said.

"You're pushy and you're a ghost," I said.

Charlotte narrowed her eyes. "Cookie Chanel, you take that back. I am very much a Southern lady."

"No arguing," Minnie warned with a wave of her finger.

I raised an eyebrow. "Fine, I take it back."

Charlotte pushed her shoulders back and held her head high. "Thank you."

"Grandma Pearl, did Tyler say anything else to you?" I asked. "How did he get in there in the first place?"

"Probably because he's not the brightest bulb in the chandelier," Charlotte said under her breath.

Minnie covered her mouth and giggled.

Tyler hissed at Charlotte. The negativity was thick in my shop today. I didn't like the way that felt.

Grandma Pearl spelled out another sentence.

He doesn't know was her response this time. That wasn't much help, but I'd have to accept it.

"Do you know anything about the murder, Grandma Pearl?" I asked.

She had great intuition and had helped with other mysteries. We waited with bated breath as she moved the planchette across the board again.

Lurking.

That was the only word that she spelled out.

"What does that mean?" Charlotte asked.

"I think she means someone is lurking around the shop. Is that right, Grandma? I bet she can sense them. You know cats can pick up on those types of things," I said.

"Yes, but she's not really a cat," Charlotte said.

"No, but it has to have some part in it. Though Grandma was always in tune with things. I guess she always had a knack for it."

"That must explain where you get your special ability," Minnie said.

Tyler jumped from the counter and Grandma Pearl followed him. They both sat at the front window now. They meowed back and forth. Apparently they really were talking to each other. Now I was left wondering what Grandma had meant by the word *lurking*. Maybe we did share the same intuition because I felt as if someone was lurking around the shop too.

I moved to the front of the store to get a better view of the street. Perhaps someone was out there. Though I thought Grandma Pearl would alert me more if I was in immediate danger. Maybe she didn't sense that much. I had to be extra careful just in case. I stopped at the door and peered outside. Nothing seemed out of the ordinary. People drove up and down the street while others strolled along the sidewalk going in and out of shops. A chill went down my spine, although I couldn't pinpoint why.

A foreboding feeling hung over my shop like a dark cloud.

"Do you see anyone?" Charlotte asked from over my shoulder.

"Nothing," I said.

"It's probably nothing," she said.

Charlotte was just trying to make me feel better. I appreciated her attempt.

"Yes, it's nothing to worry about," Minnie said with a bright smile.

She was always like a ray of sunshine. I tried to push the thoughts from my mind and get back to work. At least I had the clothing to take my mind off the murder.

The day went by rather quickly as I helped customers and sorted through inventory. I'd discovered a good collection of clothing from the 1950s at a garage sale recently. Hidden gems that the homeowners were selling for fifty cents apiece. Like the white blouse with the Peter Pan collar and tiny pearl buttons. I'd fallen in love with the pink Ethel of Beverly Hills cardigan with beading along the front. The beauty of these pieces never grew old with me. Fashion was like art for our bodies, and just because the clothing had been worn didn't mean it wasn't still art.

At the end of the workday, Heather was waiting at her shop for me. She had the place next to mine. Magic Emporium encompassed the entire bottom part of the three-story brick building. The small space was narrow, but it was the perfect size for her place. After flipping the sign to CLOSED and shutting off the lights, I locked up my shop and headed next door with two ghosts and two cats in tow. The smell of incense hit me when I walked through the door. As if on cue, Charlotte complained about it.

"Oh, that patchouli again." She waved her hand in front of her face.

I enjoyed the smell actually. It reminded me of my mother. Speaking of which, I had to call her later this evening. She expected a call from me at least every other day. My dad had a golf weekend planned. My mother had invited Heather and me to the beach for the weekend. Sadly, I'd told her I was too busy. She didn't know it was because of a murder investigation. She would tell me to keep out of it.

That was probably sound advice, but I just couldn't help myself. My father worried about me, but I knew he secretly thought my sleuthing was intriguing. I was sad that we couldn't join my mother for the weekend. I hoped to make it there soon. My mother loved Heather. She had more in common with her than me, I suppose. It was as if Heather was her long-lost daughter. My mother wasn't much into fashion. Long skirts, loose T-shirts, and Birkenstock sandals made up her outfit of the day . . . every day.

The walls in the shop were full of books on the occult and paranormal. I knew there had to be something in one of the books that would answer my questions. If not, then I held out little hope that I'd ever discover the truth. Bottles of potions and herbs filled the other nooks and crannies of the space. When Heather glanced up she waved me over. A stack of books sat on the counter in front of her.

"I pulled out as many of the books that I could find on the subject," she said as soon as we approached the counter.

"Oh, thank you, Heather. This means so much to me, and probably to Tyler too." I gestured toward the cat.

Tyler and Grandma Pearl were on the floor by my feet. They stared up at Heather.

"Charlotte, what's wrong with you?" Heather asked.

I still couldn't get used to the fact that Heather could see the ghosts.

Charlotte frowned as though she had forgotten too.

"She thinks it stinks in here," I said.

"Charlotte, it can't smell any worse than when you project your spirit perfume at us." Heather waved her hand in front of her nose.

"I'll have you know that is Chanel Number Five and it smells lovely. Doesn't it, Cookie?" Charlotte placed her hands on her hips.

I knew if I wanted to keep the peace I would have to agree with Charlotte.

"Yes, Charlotte, it is a lovely scent."

I loved the perfume too though, so it wasn't as if I was lying to her.

Heather rolled her eyes. "Okay, we'll just get right into this."

Heather opened the hardback book.

"I expected magical dust to float through the air." Charlotte grinned, as if that would make her comment less snarky.

Heather ran her index finger down the page, checking the table of contents. She flipped to a page in the middle of the book and tapped it with her finger.

"What does it say?" I asked, leaning over her shoulder to take a peek.

Charlotte and Minnie gathered close. I knew Charlotte was interested.

Heather scanned the page. "Nothing."

"Nothing? I find that hard to believe." Charlotte placed her hands on her hips.

"I'm not giving up yet, Charlotte, calm down." Heather closed the book and picked the next one off the top of the pile.

"I'm calm. I'm always calm," Charlotte said.

"Yeah, right." I laughed.

Heather flipped to another page in this book.

"Well, they have to say something." Charlotte tapped her fingers against the counter.

Heather glared at her, so Charlotte stopped.

Heather plopped the book onto the "no help" pile and the next followed that path too. There were only a couple of books left. I was starting to think this was leading nowhere. Minnie was pacing, and Charlotte was impatiently tapping her foot against the floor.

"Aha!" Heather exclaimed.

Charlotte clutched her chest. "Oh, do you have to scream out like that?"

Minnie rushed over. "What is it?"

"I think I found something." Heather tapped the page.

"What does it say?" I tried to read over her shoulder.

Heather read the page. "It says that in times of distress or a horrible passing that a spirit can become confused. The person isn't ready or doesn't know how to move on from this dimension."

I released a deep breath. "That makes sense."

"What you're saying is this was just an accident?" Charlotte asked.

"It looks that way," Heather said.

"So the cat was probably just a stray cat that was in the graveyard when Tyler was killed?" Minnie asked.

"And he moved into the body in a panic," Heather said.

"It's a good thing it was a cat. This could have been much worse. What if it had been a skunk?" Charlotte asked.

Heather laughed, which shocked Charlotte and me. This new ability that Heather had discovered had really brightened her mood. She seemed more confident too.

"So you need to figure out why Tyler was murdered and who did it. And you have to figure out the same for Minnie." Heather looked at my new ghost.

"Not only that, but I have very little to go on too," I said around a sigh.

"Oh, don't worry about me," Minnie said with a wave of her hand. "I'm fine right where I am."

Heather sat on the stool behind the counter. "Let's go over what you have so far."

I pushed the hair out of my eyes. "Tyler had an ex-girlfriend who wasn't happy with him for breaking up. Plus, there was a new woman in his life. Shanna Sizemore. I don't have information on her yet. Just what I found on his cell phone."

"How long had they been dating?" Heather asked.

"That's the thing, he had only been talking to her. There was never an actual face-to-face meeting or date."

"Interesting." Heather lifted an eyebrow. "Where does she live?"

"I haven't found that out yet, but I plan to talk with her," I said.

"Well, what are you waiting on? Let's go." Heather jumped up from the stool and grabbed her burlap tote bag.

"She told you she doesn't have her address," Charlotte said.

"Oh right," Heather said.

"I do have a phone number from Tyler's phone. It has to be hers," I said.

"And you haven't called her yet?" Heather asked.

"Well, Dylan acted as if he didn't want me to be involved in this case."

Charlotte rolled her eyes. "Since when has that ever stopped you in the past? He'll be thanking you when you solve this case."

"Charlotte has a good point," Heather said.

Charlotte smiled. "Thank you, Heather."

Charlotte and Heather being nice to each other was weird. This would take some getting used to.

"Just because I have a natural knack for the sleuthing stuff doesn't mean that I'll solve the case." I pulled out my phone and stared at the screen, hesitating before actually pressing the number.

Yes, I had saved it on my phone, so all I had to do was touch the screen and it would dial Tyler's new love interest. I suppose I knew all along that I would eventually call the number. It had to be done.

Charlotte tapped her fingers on the counter again. "What are you waiting for?"

Heather crossed her arms in front of her chest. "You need to call."

"It'll be okay to call," Minnie said in her sweet voice.

Now I had all of them pressuring me. I stared at the phone for a few seconds longer. What was I waiting for? Just because Dylan would be upset with me? Yes, I suppose that was it.

"I don't know what to say to her," I said.

"Cookie Chanel doesn't know what to say? Well, this must be a first." Charlotte tossed her hands up.

"It'll be fine," Heather said.

After releasing a deep breath, I touched the screen and it lit up. The number dialed and I listened to the rings from the other end of the line. What if she didn't answer? A couple more rings and there was still no answer.

"There's no answer," I said.

"Leave a message," Heather urged.

"Are you sure you dialed the number?" Charlotte asked with a skeptical look.

"Yes, I'm sure. It just rings. No voice mail." I ended the call.

Heather tapped her bottom lip with her index finger. "What other information about her did you find on the phone?"

"I have an email address."

"Well, send her an email," Heather said with a wave of her hand.

"What will I say? She doesn't even know me," I said.

"Good question," Heather said.

We stood around, lost in thought.

"I know," Minnie exclaimed.

We stared at Minnie, waiting for her to reveal the idea.

"Tell her about a sale at your shop. Maybe she'll come in to look around." Minnie smiled, as if this was the best idea ever.

Charlotte and Heather groaned in unison. Grandma Pearl and Tyler were so disappointed that they walked over to the door to wait for us to leave. Even they had lost hope.

"Actually, it's not a bad idea. I'll tell her that a friend told me she was looking for vintage clothing and gave me her email address."

"Yes. That is a perfect idea," Minnie said with excitement in her voice. "Not that I condone lying."

"Of course not," Charlotte said in her typical sarcastic tone.

"Shanna will want to know who the friend is that gave me her email address," I said.

"I suppose it's worth a try." Heather didn't sound convinced.

It was the only idea I had.

I typed out a quick message on my phone and hit send. "I hope she answers."

Chapter 11

Cookie's Savvy Tips for Vintage Shopping

====================

*Another thing that makes dressing in vintage so great
is you can pick out the style you love the most.
There are many decades to choose from.*

The next day I was sitting at the counter at my shop sorting through receipts. I had to admit that I was a bit down that I hadn't received a response from Shanna. It had been a long shot though. The email could have even gone to her spam filter. She probably saw that it was from a store and deleted it. At least I'd given it a try.

"Instead of moping around like a chicken when an egg broke in it, do something about this," Charlotte said as she sat on the settee.

Charlotte's long legs were stretched out across the length of the seat and her hands were propped behind her head. Sun filtered through the window, highlighting the streaks of red through Charlotte's dark hair. It looked like a glass of cola held up in the sunlight.

"What do you suggest I do? I can't make her

answer me. Maybe she doesn't even use that email address anymore. Just like she apparently doesn't use that phone number anymore. There are so many possible reasons why she didn't answer," I said.

"I think it's suspicious that she doesn't use the email address or phone number any longer after Tyler was killed." Minnie stood by the front window trying to play with the cats.

I didn't even realize she was paying attention to the conversation.

"Exactly. Good point, Minnie." Charlotte pointed.

The cats dozed in the yellowy sunshine that shone through the front window and seemed unimpressed with her efforts.

"Give me a minute . . . I'll think of something." I tapped my fingers against the counter.

Silence once again took over the room.

After a few seconds Charlotte sat up on the settee. "I got it!"

"I'm almost afraid to hear this idea," I said.

"Don't be a Negative Nancy. Would I steer you wrong?" Charlotte asked.

I quirked an eyebrow. "Yes."

She narrowed her eyes. "Are you still upset about me telling you it was a costume party? That was months ago, and I thought it was funny. You looked cute dressed as a cat."

"You went to a costume party?" Minnie turned her attention to us.

"It wasn't a costume party after all. Oops."

Charlotte leaned her head back and held her stomach as she laughed with delight over my embarrassment.

"Never mind that. I don't want to discuss it. What's your idea?" I asked.

"If Shanna was trying to date Tyler, then maybe she's on the lookout for another date now that Tyler is gone. She might not talk to a woman, but she would probably talk to a good-looking potential suitor. A real charmer," Charlotte said with a click of her tongue.

I had to admit it wasn't a terrible idea, although I didn't like deceiving someone. "Who do you have in mind? No way am I volunteering Dylan. He would never go for that."

"You don't need a guy to do it." Charlotte arched her perfectly sculpted eyebrows. "You're just talking through email. Pretend to be a guy."

"That isn't nice at all. You want me to catfish her?" I asked.

Charlotte placed her hands on her hips. "Do you want to solve this case or not? Sometimes you have to do things that aren't so nice. The world isn't always a pleasant place."

"What is catfishing?" Minnie asked.

"So you want me to toy with someone's emotions?" I asked.

"It's not like she's going to fall in love with you," Charlotte said.

"You never know . . . I am charming." I waggled my eyebrows.

Charlotte snorted. "Don't flatter yourself."

"What is catfishing?" Minnie asked.

I glared at Charlotte. "I suppose I could ask her a few questions and give her a fake name."

"No harm in that," Charlotte said with a wide devilish smile.

She was just happy because she thought she was getting her way.

"What is catfishing?" Minnie repeated with frustration.

"Tricking someone to think you're someone else," Charlotte and I said in unison.

Minnie furrowed her brow. "That's not very nice."

Charlotte clapped her hands. "Now we need to decide on a name. Since Cookie's name is Cassandra, how about Cash?"

"I didn't know your name is Cassandra," Minnie said.

"When I was a child I loved cookies, so my grandmother called me Cookie. It matched with the last name Chanel. The nickname stuck," I said.

Grandma Pearl meowed from across the room. Her eyes remained closed as she basked in the sun.

"That's a cute story. I like Cookie, but Cassandra is pretty too," Minnie said.

"You loved cookies when you were a child?" Charlotte turned to Minnie. "She still loves cookies . . . and pie, and cake."

I dismissed her comment with a wave of my hand. "*Cash*, I like it. He sounds mysterious."

"I know, right? I could totally develop the perfect

man. Now if he would just really act that way," Charlotte said.

"Well, don't make him too good. Remember I don't want her to fall in love," I said with a warning wave of my finger.

"Fine, I'll add a touch of male chauvinism," Charlotte said.

I rolled my eyes.

"Was this some kind of dating service they were using?" Charlotte asked.

"Yes, an app." I pulled out my phone.

"I'll never figure out all this lingo," Minnie said in a defeated voice.

"It's a way for people to talk to each other without making phone calls," I explained.

"So you don't actually speak?" Minnie asked.

"Not unless the people actually agree to talk to each other on the phone," I said.

"What will you do if she wants to talk on the telephone?" Minnie stared at me with wide eyes.

"I will tell her no and stop writing to her," I said.

"That sounds risky." Minnie didn't sound convinced that this was a good idea.

I filled out the necessary information to create an account. "Now what?"

Charlotte stepped closer. "You have to find a photo of a male model and add that to the profile."

"Oh, what a tangled web we weave . . ." Minnie raised an eyebrow.

"Don't listen to her," Charlotte said with a wave of her hand.

I searched for a photo. "What about this one?"

Charlotte leaned closer for a better look. "I don't like his hair."

"What about this one?" I tapped the screen.

"He has beady little eyes." Charlotte pointed.

"I don't think there was anything wrong with either of them."

Charlotte raised her eyebrows. "That's why you need me to help."

"This is wrong. I don't think you should be doing this," Minnie said.

"Don't listen to her," Charlotte said. "Wait. That man is gorgeous. Use that one."

"That is Timothy Olyphant. He's an actor. I think she'd recognize him."

"Oh," Charlotte said through pursed lips.

"What about this one?" I pointed.

Charlotte studied the screen. "I suppose he'll do. He's no Timothy whatever his name is though."

I typed on my phone. "Anything else you want me to say in the profile?"

"You don't want it to seem as if you're trying too hard," Charlotte said. "Women don't like that."

"Okay . . . so what should I write?"

"You don't want him to be too arrogant, but he shouldn't be a spineless jellyfish either." Charlotte pointed at my phone.

I rubbed my temples. "This is giving me a head-ache."

"He should like animals," Minnie said. "Men who like animals are always nice."

"That's true." Charlotte punctuated the sentence with a jab of her finger.

"How about he has a golden retriever?" I asked.

Minnie pointed. "That's good."

For someone who thought I shouldn't do this, Minnie was sure getting into devising the perfect man.

"So he should be successful, kind, and a bit mysterious." Charlotte ticked each quality off on her fingers.

"He has a lot of expectations to meet." I blew the hair out of my eyes.

Charlotte placed her hands on her hips. "He wants to get a date, doesn't he?"

I frowned. "He's not real."

"Shanna doesn't know that." Charlotte shook her head.

I typed out a few things and showed them to Charlotte. "How does that look?"

Her left eyebrow raised. "I suppose that will be fine."

"Good, because I am exhausted from trying to create this dreamboat."

"You'll see, Cookie. My guy will have a date with Shanna in no time." Charlotte pushed back her shoulders and marched across the room to the settee.

Minnie stared at me for a second before hurrying after Charlotte.

To my surprise, later that day I received a message through the dating app from Shanna.

"I have a message," I said, waving my phone through the air.

Charlotte and Minnie had been whispering in the corner of the room. I had no idea what they were discussing, but they dashed over when I announced the message. Even the cats hopped down from the windowsill and ran to the counter. I almost couldn't believe it had actually worked. Now I would have to figure out a way to ask her about Tyler.

"Ask her if she has a boyfriend?" Charlotte pointed at my phone.

I typed in the message and hit send. Within seconds Shanna replied "No."

"That's a vague answer. I need more than that," I said.

"Tell her you can't believe a pretty girl like her wouldn't have a boyfriend." Charlotte smiled widely. She was proud of her idea.

"That is so cheesy. With a pickup line like that I would never get a date with her," I said.

Charlotte quirked an eyebrow. "It is not cheesy. Just type it and I guarantee it will work."

A groan escaped my lips. "Fine. I'll write it."

Shanna responded right away with a thank-you and a smiley face.

"See, I told you it would work," Charlotte said with a smug smile.

"This is getting me nowhere. I have to ask more," I said, tapping my fingers against the counter.

"Find out if she wants to meet." Charlotte gestured toward the phone.

Minnie was pacing again. Tyler and Grandma Pearl stared at me, patiently waiting for the right outcome. Charlotte wouldn't like what I was about to say. I placed the phone down on the counter and turned to Charlotte.

"What?" she asked with a confused look.

"You can't ask a woman to meet five minutes after first starting to speak with her. Nothing says *serial killer* quite like that." I mimicked stabbing with an imaginary knife.

Charlotte pursed her lips. "I suppose I got a bit excited and wasn't thinking."

"I'll say." I picked up the phone again.

I couldn't believe that Charlotte admitted she was wrong. She rarely did that.

"Just keep talking with her and you'll eventually be able to meet her," Minnie said.

I hadn't been sure Minnie had even been listening. She'd been too busy walking back and forth.

"Yes, but how long will that take?" I asked around a sigh.

"I suppose that depends on how charming you are," Charlotte said with a click of her tongue. "Which means it could take a while."

I narrowed my eyes. "This is just all wrong. I shouldn't have done this."

"I tried to warn you that it was a bad idea," Minnie said. "However, you didn't listen to me."

"You've already started it now. No need to stop,"

Charlotte said with a wave of her hand. "It's not like you to give up."

No, I didn't usually give up, but this was one time I was seriously considering it. Shanna was asking a lot of questions. I didn't know if that was because she was interested in learning more about my fake persona or if she was suspicious. Whatever the reason, it was making me even more anxious. I spotted a customer headed for the entrance and stashed my phone in my pocket as if the person would realize what I'd been doing.

"You would make a terrible criminal," Charlotte said.

"That's a good thing," I whispered.

When the woman entered the shop, I smiled at her and said, "Welcome to It's Vintage Y'all."

I hoped I didn't sound suspicious. Charlotte walked away, shaking her head. Minnie followed her. The cats dashed toward the window. They didn't want to hang around strangers. The woman frowned when she spotted the cats dashing around the room. How would she have reacted if she'd seen the ghosts? The middle-aged brunette scanned the room. She was probably looking for more animals.

"May I help you find anything?" I asked.

"I'm just looking. Thank you." The woman headed toward a rack of dresses.

My phone alerted me to another message. Charlotte and Minnie heard the sound too. They rushed over.

"Well, what does it say?" Charlotte waved for me to check the phone.

"Yes, you can't keep us waiting," Minnie said.

"Don't worry about the customer right now," Charlotte said.

I had to worry about the customer. It was my job to help the customers. Without them I would be out of business. Charlotte knew that. She was just getting too wrapped up in the moment.

"It's from Shanna," I whispered so the customer wouldn't hear me.

"Good. Keep talking to her until you convince her to see you," Charlotte said.

"Again that sounds like a serial killer." I typed into my phone.

The customer looked my way and frowned. Oops. She must have heard me say "serial killer." That was awkward. A guaranteed way to lose a customer was to mention a lunatic murderer. Especially after there had just been a murder in town. Had the woman heard about the murder? I assumed she must be a tourist. Minnie walked from around the counter and over to the woman who was now sifting through a rack of dresses.

"What is she doing?" Charlotte asked.

I don't know, I mouthed.

Minnie had never paid much attention to the customers. Now she was standing close to the woman, studying her face.

"I'll take care of this," Charlotte said. "She's still a confused newbie ghost."

Charlotte moved over to Minnie. She reached out for Minnie and I was surprised to see that they could actually touch each other. If I tried to touch Charlotte my hand would pass right through her. Charlotte guided her back over to me.

"What was that all about?" I asked when they returned.

"That woman looks so familiar," Minnie said.

"So you thought by staring at her up close you would figure out who she is?" Charlotte placed her hands on her hips.

"Yes, I suppose I did." Minnie looked down at her shoes.

"So who is she?" I asked while watching the woman.

The customer had moved closer to the door now. She probably wanted to make her escape from the weird vintage clothing shopkeeper.

Minnie tossed her hands up. "I have no idea."

"She probably just looks like someone you used to know," Charlotte said.

The customer exited the shop without looking back at me.

"Have a nice day," I called in her wake.

Undoubtedly she never even heard my words.

"Did I chase away the customer?" Minnie frowned.

"No, she was probably just browsing," I said.

Or the customer heard me talking to myself.

That was likely the reason. Another message came from Shanna.

"She is a little clingy, no?" Charlotte said, looking over my shoulder.

"There is something odd about her," I agreed.

Chapter 12

Charlotte's Tips for a Fabulous Afterlife

Be prepared to help the living a lot. They need it.

I had set up a meeting with Shanna for the next day. The fact that she was so eager to meet a stranger made me uncomfortable. Nevertheless, I wanted to speak with her. I'd already made a plan for talking with her. Of course, she thought she was meeting a man at the diner. Charlotte had suggested I dress up as a man. I had to draw the line at that. My plan seemed much easier. I'd be there and start a casual conversation with Shanna. She'd think the guy had stood her up, and that would give me the opportunity to question her. Of course there was always the chance that she wouldn't speak with me.

I'd spent all morning at work worrying over this meeting. Now it was close to lunchtime and I headed toward the diner. The ghosts walked along beside me. Minnie always had a spring in her step, as if she was skipping through a field of wildflowers. Whereas Charlotte always looked as if she was walking the runway. Downtown was busy with people filling the sidewalks and cars buzzing up and down the main street. The ghosts and I stepped into the diner and I looked around for Shanna. So far, I didn't see anyone that looked like the photo.

Dixie walked over to me. "Good afternoon, Cookie, are you placing a to-go order or eating in?"

I was still distracted by scanning the room for Shanna. "I'll be eating here today."

"Oh, this is a real treat. Twice in just a few days you're eating in. Sit wherever you'd like, sugar. There's an available booth up at the front. Or I can clean the table back there off for you. I know you like to sit at the back so you can watch everything at the front."

"The one here at the front is fine." I managed to cast a glance at her and smile, even though I couldn't take my eyes off the door.

I took a seat at the booth toward the front of the diner so that if Shanna entered I wouldn't miss her. I could talk to her right away. The ghosts sat across from me. They helped me look around the room for Shanna.

"Do you see her?" I whispered.

Charlotte pointed. "That woman over there appears as if she is looking for someone. It kind of looks like the picture, but not exactly."

I peeked over my shoulder at the woman in the booth behind me. Just as Charlotte had said, it looked as if she was watching for someone, but there was something different about her from the photo I'd seen of Shanna.

Dixie came over to take my order. "The usual, honey?"

"I'll just have a salad and water," I said.

"You seem preoccupied. Is everything okay?" Dixie asked.

"Is there anyone here who is waiting on someone else before they order?" I asked.

Dixie gestured toward the booth behind me. "That woman said she's waiting on a blind date. She seems nervous too, poor thing."

That had to be Shanna.

"I'll go get your salad," Dixie said as she walked away.

"That is definitely not the same woman in the picture. Why does she have a different photo in the profile?" Charlotte asked. "Something seems fishy about this."

"Maybe she doesn't think she's pretty and used someone else's photo," I said.

"She's an attractive woman and the photo is similar, so that can't be it," Charlotte said with a raised eyebrow. "I say we get to the bottom of this right away."

"She's tricking you just like you tricked her," Minnie said.

"Cookie had a reason to do it. I want to know what *her* reason is." Charlotte didn't take her stare off Shanna.

"Maybe I should switch to the other side of the booth so that we are looking at each other. We'll make contact and be able to start a conversation," I said.

"Whatever you think," Charlotte said. "She might think it's strange that you switch seats just to stare at her."

"I won't stare," I whispered.

I used everything I could think of to hide when I talked to the ghosts. My phone to my ear, a napkin over my mouth, a menu over my face. If people saw me talking to myself they'd call the nearest psych ward.

The ghosts stood and I slipped to the other side of the table. Now that I sat across from her, I had a direct view of the woman. She tapped her fingers against the table. Her gaze was focused on the door. What would I say? How would I start a conversation?

Dixie brought over my salad. "Do you need anything else, Cookie?"

"I'm good," I said with a smile.

"I'll be back to talk with you in a bit. As you can see it's crazy busy right now." Dixie gestured around the room.

That was fine with me, because I didn't want to miss the woman if she got up and left. Shanna or whatever her name was. If she'd added a fake photo that certainly meant it was possible that her name wasn't really Shanna. I nibbled on my salad while I watched her.

"You're being kind of stalkerish," Charlotte said, snapping me back to attention.

I realized that my staring was a bit strange, but it was as if I couldn't take my eyes off her for a second. I knew the minute I did she would get up and leave. The woman must have felt my stare because she finally looked at me.

I smiled and said, "How are you?"

Charlotte groaned. "That's even creepier. I've seen guys in bars less creepy."

Charlotte was not helping. I wasn't good at this so she should cut me some slack.

"Fine," Shanna said with a snippy tone.

"She doesn't seem happy," Minnie said.

"Are you waiting on someone? You seem nervous." I tried to sound as friendly as possible. It was coming off weird no matter how nice I tried to be to her.

"You're digging a deeper hole," Charlotte said.

"And soon she will fall in," Minnie added.

She eyed me. "This guy was supposed to meet me."

"He's late?" I asked.

She shrugged. "I guess he's not showing up."

"Yes, guys are the worst," I said.

Charlotte said, "That's good. Bond with her over how sleazy men can be. She'll be more comfortable talking to you."

"What time was he supposed to meet you?" I asked.

She looked at her watch. "Just a few minutes ago."

"Oh well, there's still time for him to show up, I guess."

"You're just being evil now. You know good and well he isn't showing up." Charlotte laughed. "I like it."

"I suppose," Shanna said around a sigh.

"I've had terrible luck with dating," I said. "So who set you up on this blind date? A friend?"

I munched on my salad so that it would seem as if I wasn't entirely clinging on to her every word. Casually I looked at her again.

Shanna studied my face again. "Actually, we met on a dating app."

"Oh, that's interesting. Have you met many men that way?" I asked.

"Now you're back to sounding creepy," Charlotte warned.

Shanna's right eyebrow shot up. "A couple, I guess."

"See, she is suspicious." Charlotte pointed.

I couldn't see how asking if she'd used the app before would set off a red flag. No matter what Charlotte said, I was pushing forward with my questions.

"What happened with those dates?" I asked.

"I suppose they weren't good matches." Shanna focused her attention on the door again.

Did she even know what had happened to Tyler? Since she was supposed to be a stranger to me, it would be almost impossible to insert that information into the conversation.

"So what's this guy like? The one you're supposed to meet?" I asked, placing the fork full of lettuce in my mouth.

"He seemed nice," she said. "Though a little pushy."

Charlotte laughed. She was the one who had told me to ask more questions. If anyone was pushy it was Charlotte, not me. Or Cash to Shanna.

"He was probably just nervous," I said.

"Now you're defending yourself." Charlotte's laughter increased.

"Oh well, with a name like Cash I should have known he would be trouble. It's probably for the best," Shanna said with a wave of her hand.

Hey, I thought it was a good name. Minnie joined in Charlotte's merriment. I was so happy they were having a good time at my expense. I meant that in the most sarcastic way.

"What about the guy you talked to before that?" I pushed the conversation away from Cash.

"Oh, subtle," Charlotte said.

"She is talking though," Minnie said. "You have to give Cookie credit for starting a conversation."

Minnie was much better at handing out compliments than Charlotte. Plus, at least Charlotte and Minnie had mostly stopped laughing at me now. So much for moral support from those two. Next time,

I would make them wait outside for me. Though I wasn't sure how I would force them to do that.

Shanna stared at me again. "He died."

"Wow, I hadn't expected her to have such a cold expression when she said that." Charlotte rubbed her arms. "Gave me the chills. And I'm a ghost!"

"That sent a shiver down my spine," Minnie said.

I tried to act surprised. Actually, it wasn't hard because, like Charlotte said, Shanna's expression had shocked me too. I hadn't expected Shanna to be so matter-of-fact about what happened to Tyler.

After a couple seconds I got up enough nerve to ask, "What happened to him? If you don't mind me asking."

"Apparently, he was murdered," Shanna said.

"Yes, I remember hearing about that. Do they have any idea who did it?" I asked.

Charlotte chuckled. "If she finds out who you are she'll let you have it."

"I hope she never finds out," Minnie said.

How would she find out? Charlotte and Minnie were just being paranoid.

"They might suspect me." Shanna casually took a sip of water.

She acted as if we were discussing the weather. I almost choked on a piece of lettuce.

"Chew before swallowing, Cookie," Charlotte said.

"Are you all right, Cookie?" Minnie asked.

"Sorry, did that scare you?" Shanna's voice had even changed tone.

She sounded more menacing. Maybe she was just

trying to mess with me. Yes, that had to be it. She probably thought I was nosy and would have a little fun at my expense.

After a couple seconds I managed to compose myself. "Why would they suspect you? Had you met him?"

Had I just given away that I knew too much? Now I was being paranoid. It was a perfectly normal question to ask, I reminded myself.

Nonetheless, Shanna raised an eyebrow, but ultimately answered, "We were supposed to meet on the day he was murdered. Wouldn't that make me a suspect?"

Did she want me to answer truthfully? To be honest, it probably did make her a suspect. Anyone with contact with him would be a suspect. I had contact with him. Did that make me a suspect?

Shanna stood up from the table. Had I made her upset? Where was she going?

"He's not coming. I'm out of here." She rushed toward the door.

"Are you going to let her get away?" Charlotte asked.

"You have to stop her," Minnie added.

"I can't stop her," I said, holding the napkin to my mouth. "That would be too weird."

Just as she was going out she bumped into someone. Shanna didn't glance up at Dylan as she rushed out of the diner.

"Uh-oh. Now you're really in trouble," Charlotte said.

"Why am I in trouble? He doesn't know Shanna," I said into my napkin so no one would notice me talking.

"He's a detective. He knows a lot of things," Charlotte said with a click of her tongue.

"That's true. He's smart," Minnie added to the conversation.

Shanna made eye contact with Dylan. For a brief bit she was frozen. After a couple seconds she dashed out of the diner. Dylan watched Shanna before focusing on the diner again. Within seconds he spotted me. He smiled as he walked over and slid into the booth across from me. Charlotte and Minnie scrambled to get out of his way.

"If I'll let anyone have my spot, then it's Dylan," Charlotte said.

Charlotte and Minnie stood next to the table so that they could hear the conversation.

"I thought I might find you here," Dylan said.

"Yes, she is predictable," Charlotte said.

"I thought I'd stop for lunch," I said with a smile.

Did I sound suspicious? I never knew if I was hiding it. I hoped Dylan didn't know Shanna. After all, I had given him Tyler's phone. He had watched her as if he might have known her. I should tell him the truth. If I didn't then I'd be interfering with his work, right? Though he wanted me to stay out of it. I was torn and didn't know what to do.

"That sounds like a good idea. I'm starving," Dylan said.

"Does his voice sound suspicious?" Charlotte

asked. "I think he knows you were up to something other than lunch."

"Yes, I picked up on that as well," Minnie said.

Now they were making me even more anxious. I needed the ghosts to be quiet so that I could think of what to say if Dylan asked questions about Shanna. With Charlotte and Minnie that was unlikely to happen.

Dylan waved at Dixie. She came over and I figured this would give me time to plan my words.

"The usual?" Dixie asked.

Dylan gave her the thumbs-up. "He comes here just as much as you do," Charlotte said. "A match made in heaven."

"They do make a cute couple," Minnie said.

I fidgeted with the fork.

"When Cookie isn't acting suspicious they make a cute couple. Now she's just letting him know she did something. She might as well wear a big sign announcing it to the room." Charlotte waved her arm in a grand gesture.

"What's on your mind, Cookie Chanel?" Dylan asked as he studied my face.

"What makes you think there's something on my mind?" I asked with a nervous chuckle.

"The way you're pushing that lettuce around on the plate." Dylan pointed at my plate.

"That doesn't necessarily mean anything," Charlotte said. "After all, it is lettuce. Now if it had been a cheeseburger she would have scarfed it down already. What gave her away was the nervous laughter."

I glared at her.

"What? I only speak the truth." Charlotte held her hands up.

"The look on her face gives her away too." Minnie pointed. "Oh, now that scowl isn't good either."

"The ghosts are here?" Dylan asked as he looked to his left and to the right.

"Minnie and Charlotte are here." I gestured. "No new ghosts as of yet."

"Good afternoon, ladies," Dylan said with a huge smile.

The ghosts practically swooned.

"Hi, Dylan," they said in unison.

Dylan looked toward the door. "That woman that bumped into me on the way out the door . . . she was leaving in a hurry because of you, wasn't she?"

My mouth dropped. "What makes you say a thing like that?"

"You have to admit he has reasons to be suspicious," Charlotte said. "He's really good at reading you. I guess that's why he's a detective."

"Plus, it's true. The woman was leaving because of Cookie," Minnie pointed out. "I've only been here a short time and I can already see that. Cookie is bad at hiding things."

Technically Shanna was leaving because she thought she'd been stood up. I probably just sped up her desire to get out of the diner. I placed a fork full of lettuce into my mouth and chewed. This gave me time to think of something to say. Dylan was patient though and waited for me to finish. Sadly, I wasn't coming up with much in the way of excuses.

When I attempted to place more food in my mouth, he touched my arm and chuckled. "Nice try, Cookie. Now spill it. What was going on between you and that woman?"

"Oh, you're being interrogated by the police," Charlotte said. "This is better than a Lifetime Movie."

"Well, she was at the scene of the crime. They usually interview suspects, er, I mean witnesses," Minnie added.

They weren't helping matters.

I wiped my mouth with a napkin. "Okay, here's the thing . . . she was the woman who was supposed to meet Tyler the day he was murdered."

Dylan's eyes widened. "How do you know this?"

"Oh, this will be a tricky question to answer," Charlotte said.

Minnie leaned against the booth. "You'll have to tell the truth. I hope he doesn't take you to jail. I wouldn't know how to get you out."

There was only one thing to do. I had to answer truthfully. A flash of being behind bars popped into my head. It wasn't a pleasant scene.

"I tricked her into thinking I was a guy so she would come here to the diner and speak with me." The words rushed out. "I just wanted answers about how she knew Tyler and what their relationship was like."

"So that's why she stormed out?" Dylan asked.

"No, she never knew I was the guy. I let her believe that the guy stood her up. After that I talked about how sleazy men are," I said with a wave of my hand.

Dylan stared at me. "I'm not sleazy."

"You really put your foot in your mouth now," Charlotte said.

"Oh, I think you hurt his feelings," Minnie said.

"Of course not, but I just told her what she wanted to hear." I smiled, hoping that would make Dylan not upset with me.

"What did you find out?" Dylan asked.

"Other than that she was supposed to meet Tyler on the day he was murdered, nothing," I said around a sigh.

"I need to track her down. We've been unable to find any information on anyone with the name Shanna Sizemore," Dylan said.

"Maybe she was using a fake name," Charlotte said.

"Charlotte thinks maybe she was using a fake name," I said, relaying the message.

"That's quite possible," Dylan said.

"I can send a message to her again through the dating app. As the guy she was supposed to meet, of course," I said.

Dylan lifted an eyebrow. "What was the name of this fictitious guy?"

"Cash," I said.

Dylan chuckled. "Sounds like a guy from a romance novel."

Charlotte laughed.

Chapter 13

Cookie's Savvy Tips for Vintage Shopping

===

Don't like the current fashion trends?
Check out vintage clothing shops for
the styles that made you happy.

That evening I was home and in bed when the crash sounded from somewhere outside my bedroom door. I froze with the covers up under my chin. I knew I had to check it out, but my fear had paralyzed me.

"Don't worry, Cookie, I'll go check it out. Don't move," Charlotte whispered, as if someone would hear her.

"I hope it's not the killer," Minnie whispered.

I glared at her.

"Sorry," she said.

Charlotte disappeared out the door. I contemplated calling Dylan. What if the noise was nothing? I wouldn't want to disturb him and make him think I was completely paranoid. What was taking Charlotte so long? Minnie had followed along behind Charlotte, leaving me alone to worry about what was happening. After she'd put even more panicked thoughts in my head. I decided to stop being a chicken and go check it out for myself.

I eased out of bed and over to the bedroom door. Pressing my ear up to the wood I listened, but there were no sounds. Not even a noise from the ghosts. Releasing a deep breath, I wrapped my hand around the doorknob and twisted. I eased the door open and peeked out into the hallway. Of course it was dark. I should have left a night-light on out there.

Charlotte and Minnie were nowhere in sight. I tiptoed through the hallway and into the living room, trying not to bump into furniture. Where were Grandma Pearl and Tyler? Normally Wind Song slept at the foot of my bed. Chills traveled down my spine. Where were Charlotte and Minnie? Panic was starting to settle in. If I didn't find them in the kitchen I would have to check outside. I supposed I needed to look out there anyway. Maybe Charlotte and Minnie had stepped out there to have a look around the house. Now that I thought about it, maybe looking outside wasn't really necessary. When I reached the kitchen, I saw Charlotte and Minnie standing by the back door. They were whispering to each other and hadn't noticed that I was standing there.

"What's going on, y'all?" I asked.

Charlotte screeched and jumped. Minnie screamed.

"Don't sneak up on us like that," Charlotte said,

clutching her chest. "You nearly scared a ghost to death."

I raised an eyebrow. "What's happening in here?"

Charlotte and Minnie stepped away from the back door. Shards of glass covered the floor. The window of the back door had been broken from the outside. Panic surged through me. Was someone in the house?

"It was like that when we got in here," Charlotte said.

"Do you think someone is in the house?" I whispered.

"The door was still closed. You'd better call Dylan just to be safe." Charlotte motioned for me to move.

I rushed for my phone and dialed Dylan. It was the middle of the night, so I hoped he answered. Dylan answered after only a couple rings. Of course panic filled his voice.

"Someone broke my back door window," I whispered. "The door in the kitchen. I don't know if someone is in the house."

"I'm on my way," Dylan said.

He ended the call. What would I do until he arrived? I had to find the cats.

"I should check the rest of the house, right?"

Charlotte nodded in agreement, but Minnie shook her head no.

"Be careful," Minnie said as she tiptoed behind me. "What if someone is in here?"

Sometimes the ghosts forgot they were ghosts. My house was small, so there wouldn't be a lot to search through. Tiptoeing through the house, I checked the other bedroom, the closets, and bathrooms. Nothing seemed out of place. Why would someone break the window? There was no way I was going outside to look around. Not now. Maybe once daylight broke.

The house was still dark. I was worried if I turned on the lights the person outside might come back. I eased back down the hallway with a plan to head toward the kitchen. Something jumped out at me and I screamed. Charlotte and Minnie screamed too. I ran down the hallway so quickly that my feet got ahead of me. I tumbled face-first onto the hardwood floor. When I looked back to see who had reached for me, I saw glowing yellow eyes staring back at me.

"Tyler? Why did you do that?" I asked.

"He is just trying to be difficult," Charlotte said as she clutched her chest.

"If I wasn't dead already I surely would be now after that," Minnie said. "Are you all right, Cookie?"

I climbed up from the floor and to my feet. "I'm fine."

Grandma Pearl meowed. She was sitting at the living room's threshold.

"Where have you two been?" I asked.

I wouldn't get an answer unless I used the Ouija board. There was no time for that now.

"I hope Dylan gets here soon," Charlotte said.

Tyler ran past me, joining Grandma Pearl. As I neared them, they took off toward the kitchen.

"I think they've been in to something they shouldn't have," Charlotte said.

"Do you think they broke the door?" Minnie asked.

"I don't think that's possible," I said.

The ghosts and I hurried back toward the kitchen. I had just reached the doorway when a rattling noise caught my attention.

"Please let that be a mouse," Minnie said.

"Well, it's certainly not Mickey," Charlotte said. "I doubt there are mice in the house with two cats. Actually, I take that back. Pearl would never go after a mouse."

Grandma Pearl meowed and Tyler shook his head. Minnie clutched the back of my pajama top. The cold from her nearness sent prickles along my skin. Somehow I mustered up enough courage to continue my journey to the kitchen. However, I froze when I reached the kitchen entrance. A bright light shone on me from outside the door. My breath caught in my throat.

"Cookie, it's me," Dylan said, moving the flashlight off me. "Are you all right?"

His face came into view now. Though it was still dark. I couldn't make out anything behind him. His dark hair was tousled as if he'd just rolled out of bed. Probably because I'd dragged him away from home in the middle of the night. He wore a white T-shirt and blue shorts.

I released a deep breath. "I'm better now."

"This is almost more stress than I can handle." Minnie twisted her hands.

"You'll get used to the stress while hanging around Cookie," Charlotte said with a dismissive flick of her wrist.

"Other officers are on their way to check for fingerprints," Dylan said as he shone the light around the edges of the broken window. "I don't see anyone suspicious out here."

"That's a relief," I said, releasing a deep breath.

"I'll come around to the front door. I don't want to disturb the scene," Dylan said.

I raced to the front door and unlocked it, letting Dylan in. He'd slipped into his sneakers with no socks.

"At least he didn't come in his boxer shorts," Charlotte said, eyeing Dylan up and down.

"I'll check the rest of the house," Dylan said when he stepped inside the front hallway.

"I already did that," I said.

He frowned. "Why would you do that?"

I shrugged. "Boredom?"

"Well, for my peace of mind I'll look again. The officers should be here soon." He headed down the hallway.

"I'll wait here for them," I said.

I watched out the window waiting for the officers to arrive. After a couple seconds staring out into the darkness, I thought better of peering out the window. What if the person who broke the window was still out there and looking in at me? Thinking about some creepy person staring back at me chilled me to the bone.

Dylan emerged from the back of the house. "No one there."

"You already told him that," Charlotte said.

"Yes, but like you said, he wanted to check for himself," Minnie reminded Charlotte.

"He's as stubborn as Cookie." Charlotte trailed along after Dylan.

"I want a closer look at that window." Dylan headed for the kitchen.

I started to follow him, but the sound of police arriving pulled my attention back to the front window. Rushing over to the door, I opened it and allowed them in. Two officers in uniforms stood in front of me.

"Good evening, ma'am," the young officer said with a nod of his head.

"Dylan, er, Detective Valentine is in the kitchen." I pointed in that direction.

I followed them to the kitchen. The officers got to work right away with checking for fingerprints. Dylan walked over to me as I stood by the kitchen entrance.

"Why did someone do this?" I asked.

"My guess is they were going to break in, but something scared them away." Dylan ran his hand through his hair.

The thought sent a shiver down my spine. What-ever had stopped the person I was thankful for it.

Dylan looked around to make sure no one was listening. "Do you think the ghosts chased them away?"

I shook my head. "The ghosts were in the bedroom with me. At least I think they were. I saw Charlotte there."

Charlotte and Minnie nodded.

"Yes, they were in there with me," I said.

Dylan pushed the hair away from my face. "Try not to worry too much. Someone was probably just looking for items to steal."

"Don't worry about a thief?" Charlotte raised her voice.

"This is upsetting." Minnie stood next to me again.

The cool air made the skin of my arm prickle.

"More than likely they'll never return," Dylan said.

"More than likely?" Charlotte's voice grew louder.

"Oh, please don't let them return." Minnie shivered with fear.

"We'll get any fingerprints we can and see if we get a match," Dylan said.

He had no idea that the ghosts were upset with his comments.

"I just hope they find something," I said around a yawn.

"You should go back to bed and get some rest," he said.

There was no way I'd be able to go back to sleep.

Besides, it was now four in the morning. Soon the sun would peek out over the horizon. My next-door neighbor's rooster would announce the start of the day. That was better than any alarm clock I could buy. Though unfortunately there was no snooze button.

Dylan must have read my mind. "It looks as if you're not ready to go back to sleep. Would you like to get breakfast? It'll take your mind off things."

Though I wasn't sure I would be able to eat, it would probably distract me.

"I'd like that," I said. "Just let me get dressed."

"I'll be here in the kitchen." Dylan kissed my forehead.

My thoughts raced as I headed for the shower. I still didn't know why the person had run away. Unless the police recovered fingerprints I might never know. Although I wasn't sure that they wouldn't return. Dylan was finishing up with the other officers so I had to hurry and dress for breakfast.

When I stepped out of the bathroom I found Wind Song sitting on the upholstered chair in the bedroom by the window. She meowed at me. There was something on the chair beside her. Tyler sat on the floor beside the chair, peering up at Grandma Pearl.

"What is that?" I asked as I stepped closer.

I knew that Grandma Pearl was the one meowing at me. Wind Song rarely got a chance to say anything with Grandma Pearl in control. Plus, the twinkle in the cat's eye gave it away. I'd learned to pick up on the different mannerisms between Wind Song and my grandmother too.

"What did the cat get into this time?" Charlotte placed her hands on her hips.

"I'm just glad it's not a mouse," Minnie said.

I reached down and picked up the piece of fabric from the chair. The edges were jagged, but it had a hem.

"This looks like a piece of someone's pants." I held up the cloth.

"Did she raid your closet?" Charlotte asked. "Maybe Tyler did it. That seems like something he would do."

Tyler hissed at Charlotte.

"Bad kitty," Minnie warned with a wave of her finger.

"I do think it was Grandma Pearl," I said.

Grandma Pearl would never rip any of my clothing. She'd loved fashion as much as I did. Wind Song never did anything like that either. Tyler I didn't know well enough. Plus, he seemed like he would do something if he was mad. Examining the fabric closer, I realized it wasn't from any clothing I owned. As much as I loved clothing, I had a mental inventory of everything I owned and the clothing that was in my shop.

"Where did you get this, Grandma?" I asked, waving the fabric through the air.

She meowed.

"Unless you speak cat, you're not getting an answer right now," Charlotte said.

I suppose I'd have to wait until I got to the shop and have her use the Ouija board.

"What if she got it from the person who broke the window?" Minnie asked.

"You now, she may have a point," Charlotte said.

"That's the only way to explain it, right?" I asked. "Grandma Pearl, did you chase away the bad person?"

She meowed. How would I explain this to Dylan?

I hurried and dressed in a black, tailored Armani dress. It had a white bib collar with gold buttons that ran the length of the front of the dress. Matching gold buttons were on the cuffs. I studied my reflection. I couldn't get over how classic and professional looking this outfit made me feel. My black Mary Jane heels were trimmed in contrast white ribbon. The strap fastened with a tiny white bow.

"Now that's something I would wear. Mind if I borrow it?" Charlotte stood behind me.

"No, not at all as long as you wait until I'm not wearing it. I don't want to be twins."

"As if," Charlotte said.

I hated to leave Grandma and Tyler here while I went to breakfast, but I didn't think Dylan would understand why I had to bring the cats. It was one thing to tell him I saw and talked with ghosts, but to tell him my grandmother was stuck in the cat's body? He'd have me committed to the nearest insane asylum.

"Grandma Pearl, I'll be back soon," I whispered.

I suppose if she chased off the bad person once she could do it again if they returned. I carried the fabric out into the hallway where Dylan was waiting for me.

He smiled. "Gorgeous, as always."

"Thank you." Heat rushed to my cheeks.

My heart went pitter-pat when he complimented me. What girl didn't like a kind word? Now I had to explain this weird piece of pant leg I'd discovered.

"Once the guys are finished we can go." He motioned. "Though I feel underdressed now."

Dylan usually had on slacks and a dress shirt for work.

"Oh, wait. I have those jeans that I repaired for you. I'll go get them."

I hurried back to the bedroom and grabbed the pants. Grandma Pearl had taught me how to use a needle and thread pretty well. That skill came in handy when working with vintage clothing. There was always a button that needed sewn back on or a hemline coming loose.

When I returned to the living room I handed Dylan the jeans. "As good as new."

He took them from me. "You didn't have to do this. I could have taken them to the sewing shop in town."

I waved my hand. "I wanted to do it. No need to take them just for that little repair."

He smiled. "Well, thanks again. I'll go change."

Dylan headed down the hallway to the bathroom while I watched the officers move around the kitchen. It looked as if they were packing up their stuff.

"What will you do with that gaping hole in the door?" Charlotte asked.

"I'll have to ask someone to replace the door for me. In the meantime, I have an extra board in the shed that we can nail up there."

"I hope by 'we' you mean you and Dylan, because I don't think I'd be of any help," Charlotte said.

I chuckled. "Yes, I mean Dylan."

"What about me?" he asked as he stepped in the room.

He had changed into the jeans. He looked equally great in jeans and a T-shirt.

"I was discussing placing a board over the broken window until I can have it replaced."

"The stuff is in the shed, right?" Dylan asked.

"Yes," I said.

"I'll have it fixed in no time," he said.

"There was one other thing I wanted to talk about before we do that," I said.

Dylan studied my face. "What's that?"

I showed Dylan the fabric. "I found this in the bedroom. I think the cat found it. This isn't mine."

Dylan took the clothing. "You think it was from the person who broke the window?"

"Yes, I believe so. They must have gotten caught

somewhere and ripped their pants. I guess Wind Song found it and brought it to me."

This way I didn't have to tell him that the cat probably ripped the fabric from the person's pant leg.

Dylan quirked an eyebrow. "That is one clever cat."

I chuckled nervously. "Yes, she is special."

"We're all finished here," the officer said as they headed for the front door.

Dylan walked with them and I stepped into the kitchen to clean up the mess. I'd just finished sweeping when Dylan appeared at the back door with the board for the broken window.

I jumped and clutched my chest. "Sorry, I guess I'll still a little on edge."

Dylan opened the door and stepped into the kitchen. "We're all set. I can come over later and hang the new door."

"I don't want you to have to do that. I figured I can give it a shot myself."

Charlotte snorted. "You're handy with clothing, not home repair."

I was handy with whatever I set my mind to, although I would admit I'd probably need help. The door would be heavy.

"How about I come over to help?" Dylan asked. "It's the least I can do for you fixing my jeans."

I smiled. "Okay, that sounds fair."

"We'll be back, Grand . . . I mean, Wind Song, and other kitty," I said as we headed for the door.

Dylan gave me a strange look. I hoped he wasn't

on to me. How would I even begin to explain what had happened with the cats? Dylan and I left the cats and headed for breakfast. I tried not to worry about what had happened, but that was impossible. Of course the ghosts were in the car with us. They discussed the break-in, which didn't help ease my anxiety.

Chapter 14

Charlotte's Tips for a Fabulous Afterlife

Some ghosts are more excited than others.
Learn to be cool in the afterlife too.

After breakfast I couldn't wait to get to the shop. I wanted to get the Ouija board and see what the cats had to say about the broken window and the mystery piece of fabric. Dylan had taken me back to my house and I'd picked up the cats. Now we hurried through the door and I made a beeline for the board that was stashed under the counter.

"This is exciting," Minnie said.

"You think everything is exciting," Charlotte said. "You are even giddy when Cookie takes us to the grocery store."

"There's a lot to look at," Minnie said in a pouty voice.

I pulled out the board and placed it on top of the counter. "Okay, Grandma Pearl and Tyler, please tell us what you know."

The cats jumped onto the counter. They stared at each other. "I think they're trying to decide who should go first," I said.

"Well, someone needs to talk," Charlotte said in frustration.

After a couple more seconds Grandma Pearl reached out and moved the planchette with her graceful paw.

"I can't wait to see what they have to say," Minnie said.

She was practically jumping up and down with anticipation.

I followed Grandma Pearl's movements around the board, keeping track of the letters.

"What is she spelling?" Minnie asked.

"*Don't know,*" I said.

"What do you mean you don't know?" Charlotte asked. I thought you were keeping track of the letters. Do I have to do everything around here?"

"What I mean is she spelled out the words '*Don't know,*'" I said.

"How can she not know? They were there when the person broke the window," Charlotte said.

"We were there too and we don't know," Minnie said.

"Oh yes, I suppose you make a valid point," Charlotte said through pursed lips.

"Wait, she has more to say." I pointed at Grandma Pearl as she moved the planchette again.

"Maybe she remembered something," Minnie said.

"I hope it's something good," Charlotte added.

I waited with bated breath as Grandma Pearl spelled out other words. Tyler meowed as if he was reminding Grandma Pearl about something else that had happened.

"*Chased away?*" I repeated the message. "You chased away the person? Good job, Grandma Pearl. What did the person look like? Did you recognize the person?"

"Slow down with the questions," Charlotte said. "You're asking so many that she can't keep up."

"Sorry," I said. "Did you recognize the person? There, I condensed the questions."

"Perfect." Charlotte winked.

Again Grandma Pearl swirled the planchette around the board.

"*It was dark. Don't know how to use these cat eyes well in the dark,*" I repeated her message.

"Aren't cats supposed to be able to see in the dark?" Charlotte asked.

"I have no idea," I said.

"Actually cats have better night vision than humans. It's because of the higher numbers of rods in their retina," Minnie said.

Charlotte and I stared at Minnie.

"How did I know that?" Minnie asked with wide eyes.

"I have no idea," Charlotte said.

"So Grandma Pearl doesn't know how to use those rods?" I asked. "Was the person male or female, Grandma Pearl?"

Grandma Pearl answered. *Female.*

"So the woman was wearing the fabric. How did

you get it? Did she get her pants leg caught on something?" I asked.

We watched as Grandma Pearl spelled out her answer. *I grabbed her pant leg with my mouth and ripped it off.*

My eyes widened. "Grandma Pearl!"

Charlotte laughed. "Can you imagine what the woman was thinking when this cat attacked her?"

"I bet she was thinking don't mess with Cookie Chanel's cat," Minnie said.

"Grandma Pearl always was feisty when you made her mad," I said. "I remember the time she hit a man on the head with her pocketbook because he was getting fresh."

Charlotte held her stomach and laughed.

Grandma Pearl spelled out a response. *He wouldn't take no for an answer.*

"Good for you, Grandma Pearl," Minnie said.

"So we know it was a woman wearing pants," I said.

"That narrows it down a lot," Charlotte said.

"It may not be a great clue, but at least Grandma Pearl chased the person away. Thank you, Grandma Pearl. You saved me."

Had she saved me from the killer? The thought sent a shiver down my spine. The cats jumped down, and I put the board back under the counter.

"I could have saved you from the killer too, you know?" Charlotte said.

"Really?" I said.

"Yes, I was keeping guard in the bedroom."

I smiled to myself.

"That's important too," Charlotte added.

"Yes, it's extremely important," I said.

"Someone has to watch out for you," Charlotte said.

"That's my job." Minnie's eyes widened. "I mean, that's what I want to do. Help Cookie."

Charlotte stared at Minnie. "You're one strange ghost."

Minnie chuckled. "I suppose I am."

Charlotte and Minnie huddled in the corner of the room. They were whispering. Every few seconds they would look over at me.

"What are you all up to?" I asked.

Charlotte gave me a wide-eyed look. "What makes you think we're up to something?"

"You're whispering. That always gives it away," I said.

"That doesn't mean anything." Charlotte scoffed.

"But you told me to keep my voice down so that Cookie doesn't hear us," Minnie said.

I narrowed my eyes at Charlotte. "Not up to something, huh?"

"You talk too much, kid," Charlotte said. "You need to learn to filter what you say."

"Sorry," Minnie said.

"Okay, tell me what you have planned." I placed my hands on my hips.

"We're just discussing helping you." Charlotte waved her hand as a signal that I shouldn't ask more questions.

I quirked an eyebrow. "I'm not sure I believe you. Just don't get any crazy ideas."

"Never." Charlotte smiled.

Now that we'd talked to the cats I got down to work. There was a lot to do. I had to add clothing to the racks, work on invoices, and plan out future window displays. I was placing a stunning deep green–colored silk Dior gown on a mannequin. The sleeveless V-neck came down to a fitted drop waist and fell into soft pleats. When I'd found the dress the pleats had been losing their shape, but I'd managed to get them back with a little bit of work. Now it was as good as new.

"That would be perfect with pearls," Charlotte said.

Minnie clutched her necklace.

"Don't worry, Minnie. I didn't mean your necklace." Charlotte pretended to fan Minnie with her hand.

I'd just fastened the back of the dress when the realization hit me. I knew exactly where the fabric had come from. The thought sent a shiver down my spine. It had come from a pair of pants that I'd given Tyler for the photo shoot. Plus, I'd never received the plaid wool Ralph Lauren pants back. Did the killer have the pants? Sometimes a murderer liked to keep a memento from the crime. That meant it had to be someone with access to the clothing from the photo shoot. One of the models, perhaps? What would I do now?

"What's on your mind, Cookie? I know you have

something cooking in that head. I can tell by the look on your face." Charlotte crossed the floor and stood in front of me with her hands on her hips.

"I know where the fabric came from," I said in an excited voice.

"Where?" Minnie raced over.

"They were part of the clothing I gave to Tyler for the photo shoot. I remember it now. Plus, those pants were never returned to me. You know what this means, don't you?" I asked.

Minnie played with the pearl necklace around her neck. "No, what does it mean?"

"The killer had access to the clothing. It had to be one of the models," I said.

Charlotte held up her hand. "Not so fast. It could have been anyone who was on that photo shoot that morning. There were assistants, the boyfriend, and who knows who else Tyler came in contact with before he reached the photo shoot that morning. You gave him the clothing the day before the photo shoot. Remember?"

I placed my hand on my hip. "Way to burst my sleuthing bubble, Charlotte."

"Just stating the facts, dear, just stating the facts . . . I will admit it is highly suspicious though. Good work on remembering the clothing," Charlotte said.

"I never forget a piece of vintage." I finished the mannequin and moved to the counter. "Next, I think I need to find out who had access to the clothing."

"That sounds like a difficult task," Minnie said around a sigh.

"No one said solving a murder case was easy," I said with a click of my tongue. "It has to be done though."

Grandma Pearl meowed, capturing my attention. Or was it Wind Song this time?

"What is it, Grandma Pearl?" I asked.

She made the loud noise again. Since she didn't move from her spot at the window I figured she wanted me up there for some reason.

"I'm coming," I said.

"Your grandmother always was sassy, you said," Charlotte remarked, following me to the window.

I peered out onto the street. It was the typical scene with cars passing by and people strolling the sidewalks. One thing stood out though. Over on the sidewalk, in front of the Much Ado about Books, I spotted Ken and Heather talking. Heather was doing that thing where when she talks with guys she shuffles her foot and looks down. That was odd. She only did that when she had a crush on someone. If she had a crush on Ken she would certainly tell me.

"What are they up to?" Charlotte asked.

Minnie squeezed in between Charlotte and me for a better look. "What is it? What's happening?"

"I guess they're just talking. Don't be so suspicious," I said.

Charlotte scoffed. "As if you're not suspicious too."

"I'll admit I'm mildly curious, but that's it. Heather would tell me if there was something to tell."

"Grandma Pearl wanted you to know about it," Minnie said.

Nevertheless, I continued to watch Heather and Ken. What were they talking about that was so funny? A few more seconds and they broke up the conversation. Ken walked away and Heather hurried across the street toward her shop. Wasn't she coming in to tell me what they'd talked about? Ken looked back for another glance at Heather.

"Aren't you going to ask her what is up with them?" Charlotte asked.

"Yes, you should ask," Minnie said.

"If she wants me to know she'll tell me," I said with a wave of my hand.

"I give her less than a day until she asks Heather about this," Charlotte said, looking at Minnie. "Oh wait, I can ask her now. She can see and hear me."

Charlotte marched toward the door. I tried to move in front of her, but she passed right through me.

"Don't you dare," I said.

"And why not?" Charlotte raised an eyebrow.

"Because I don't want her to think I was spying on her."

"You were spying on her," Charlotte said.

"Yes, but I don't want her to know that."

Charlotte groaned. "Fine."

"And don't walk through me like that. It creeps me out," I said.

"Don't step in front of me and I won't have to." Charlotte frowned.

"Maybe they're throwing you a surprise birthday party, Cookie. When's your birthday?" Minnie asked.

"February twenty-sixth."

"Pisces . . . that explains a lot." Charlotte studied her fingernails.

"Since when do you know about signs?" I asked.

Charlotte shrugged but didn't comment.

"Oh, guess it's not a birthday party. Too bad for you. A party would have been fun," Minnie said with disappointment in her voice.

Tyler meowed, grabbing my attention. He'd been so quiet that I had almost forgotten he was here.

"What is it, Tyler? Is something wrong?"

Should I try to get him to use the Ouija board again? He hadn't seemed interested earlier when Grandma Pearl had used the board.

"Maybe he wants more of that delicious cat food," Charlotte said.

Tyler hissed at her.

"He's so testy." Charlotte shook her finger at him.

"I wouldn't do that if I were you, Charlotte. He may bite your finger," Minnie said.

"What is it, Tyler?" I asked again. "What do you have to tell me?"

He jumped up on the counter. Charlotte and I exchanged a look.

"Seems like he wants to talk now." I hurried over to the counter and grabbed the board.

"It's about time," Charlotte said. "He's a lazy cat."

Tyler hissed and swiped his claws toward Charlotte.

"He can hear you," I whispered.

"That's why I said it." Charlotte lifted an eyebrow.

"Okay, never mind that. Tyler, what do you want to tell us?" I asked.

Grandma Pearl had joined him on the counter now. She stared at the board, as if overseeing Tyler's message. Tyler yawned, after which he slowly placed his paw on the planchette.

"He doesn't seem that interested, so it can't be anything important," Charlotte said.

Tyler obviously took offense at Charlotte's comment. Now he moved his paw around the board at a rapid speed. He moved so quickly that it was hard to keep track of the letters.

"Slow down, cat," Charlotte said.

Somehow I'd managed to keep up.

When he'd finished the first word, Minnie gasped. "*Beware.*"

"What should I beware of?" I asked.

"If he makes some sarcastic remark . . ." Charlotte said.

Tyler moved the planchette again. The next message was two words. *Back door.*

"Beware of the back door?" I asked.

"What does that mean?" Minnie asked.

A rattling noise captured our attention. My heart sped up. The sound came from the back of the shop. At the back door to be specific.

"I hope that's a mouse," Minnie said.

"It was something bigger than a mouse," Charlotte said.

That was what I was afraid of. Someone could be at the back door. And that someone could be the killer.

"I suppose I should check it out," I whispered.

Chapter 15

Cookie's Savvy Tips for Vintage Clothing Shopping

*Some trends for seasons never go out of style
and you can always find great vintage pieces
to put those styles into your wardrobe.
Plaids for fall, wools for winter, floral prints
for spring, and bright colors for summer.*

My heart beat faster and anxiety raced through my body. No one else volunteered to check it out. I inched toward the door, reminding myself to breathe. The last thing I needed was to hyperventilate. The ghosts followed right behind me. After them were the cats. Everyone was too chicken to go first. That left me to do the dirty work.

I stopped at the door that led to the back storage room. No other noise had come from the area, but that didn't mean someone wasn't on the other side of the door waiting for me. My heart sped up as I wrapped my hand around the doorknob. I looked back at Charlotte, and she motioned for me to open the door. I released a deep breath and turned the knob. So far no one had jumped out at me.

Why hadn't I left the lights on back here? I

supposed I was trying to save on the electric bill. The back door that led out into the parking area of the shop was still closed. I wasn't sure if that made me feel much better though. The person could have closed the door once they were inside the building. What was I thinking? Just because the cat had given me a warning didn't mean someone was back here. He could have been warning me of a mouse for all I knew. Though a mouse probably wouldn't have made a noise that loud.

"What are you waiting for, Cookie? Go in there and check it out," Charlotte said.

"I'm going," I whispered.

"Yeah, Charlotte, don't get your bloomers in a bunch," Minnie said.

Even though the room was small, the walk over to the back door seemed longer than ever now. I forced my legs to move and stepped into the room. The light switch was on the opposite wall for some reason. A design flaw from whoever installed the electric. I'd meant to have it changed but never gotten around to it. I'd move it to the top of my to-do list.

Halfway across the room someone grabbed me. It was dark so I couldn't get a good look at the person. The person was trying to drag me across the room toward the back door. I stumbled backward, trying to grab the person's arms. I wanted to break free from the hold.

"Cookie, what's happening?" Charlotte screeched.

"Get off her," Minnie yelled.

I'd never heard Charlotte so panicked. I had no idea what was happening. Someone was trying to kidnap me. Was this the killer? It had to be the killer. I had to fight this person off. No longer able to balance, I fell to the floor, but the person still had a tight grip on me.

"Cookie, what can I do?" Charlotte asked.

I wasn't sure there was anything Charlotte could do. Though I suppose something was better than nothing. My thoughts raced as I tried to figure out a way to escape.

"Throw something," I yelled.

Perhaps if Charlotte moved something it would distract the person long enough for me to get away. Not the best plan, but I had to try something. By the height and size, I assumed this was a man, but I couldn't be sure. As I twisted my body and shoved, I was helpless to break free. The person had me at the back door now. Once they got me outside it would probably be all over for me. If they shoved me in a car and drove me somewhere, my chances of escaping would be slim.

With one hand still holding me, the person managed to get the door open. Light streamed through the area. I tried to turn my head to see who this was, but the person had a dark mask covering their face.

"Charlotte, do something." I kicked and attempted to move my arms.

A red high heel shoe whizzed by my kidnapper's head, narrowly missing me. As I'd hoped, his grip around me loosened. I broke free and ran for the other side of the room. I didn't bother to look back and see if my attacker was coming after me. That would only slow me down.

"Cookie, the person took off out the back door. You can stop running now."

I heard Charlotte, but I wasn't completely convinced. Better safe than sorry. I needed to call Dylan. I didn't slow down as I raced out of the back room and through the shop. If I reached the sidewalk outside I'd be safe. At least I hoped so. I didn't think a person would try to kidnap me with so many other people around. What if the attacker was looking for another victim now? I worried about Heather. I had to check on her. Once I reached the front door of the shop, I peeked over my shoulder.

With my hand on the doorknob, I paused. "Do you think the person will come back?"

"I don't know, but you should call the police right away," Charlotte said.

Sadly I didn't have my phone with me. I ran for my cell phone that I'd left on the counter. With a shaky hand I picked it up. I touched the screen and dialed Dylan's number. Thank goodness he answered right away.

"Dylan, someone broke into the shop and tried to kidnap me," I said breathlessly.

"What?" The tone of his voice sounded stunned.

I was just as shocked too.

"This is no joke. I think it was the killer," I said. "Thank goodness I got away. Though I'm worried he might return to finish the job."

"I'm on my way," Dylan said.

This was the second time within hours that Dylan had to come to my aid. It couldn't be helped though. This was serious. What would I do until he arrived? I was afraid that the person would come back. I stood by the front door with my hand on the phone in case I needed to call again. What good would that do though? Dylan was already on his way. He couldn't drive any faster. I dialed Heather's number and thank goodness she answered right away.

"Hey," she said in a cheery tone.

"Where are you?" I asked in a still panicked tone.

"I went to Office Depot for supplies."

I released a deep breath. At least I knew she wasn't at her shop. I was afraid the killer might still be around back waiting for someone to come out.

"Stay away from your shop until I tell you it's safe," I said.

"Cookie, you're freaking me out right now. What's wrong?" Heather asked. "Are you all right?"

"I'm fine, but someone attacked me in the shop."

"Oh my gosh. I'm coming there right now."

"No, don't do that. Dylan is on his way."

The ghosts and the cats stood beside me. It was nice knowing that I wasn't completely alone. I convinced Heather to stay away from her shop until I called her and said it was safe. Well, she had promised not to come, and she usually kept her promises. I hoped this time wouldn't be any different.

A couple more seconds passed and Dylan's car

screeched to a halt in front of the shop. A second later and multiple other police cars pulled along the street in front of the shop too. I raced out the door to meet Dylan.

"Thank goodness the police are here. Maybe they will find this creep," Charlotte said.

"It was so scary," Minnie said.

He embraced me in a hug. "What happened?"

"Someone was in the back room. They grabbed me and tried to pull me out the back door," I said breathlessly.

Dylan instructed the other officers to check around the building.

"Stay here with her, okay?" Dylan asked one of the officers.

The cop nodded.

"I'll be right back, Cookie." Dylan ran inside.

Of course I assumed the attacker was long gone. However, with any luck, the person left a clue. I'd recently installed a surveillance camera in the shop. I had my fingers crossed that the cameras had picked up an image of my attacker.

"I think the person who attacked you was the killer," Charlotte said.

Her words sent a shiver down my spine. Unfortunately, I'd come to the same conclusion.

"Why come after Cookie?" Minnie asked.

"They must think she's getting too close to solving the case," Charlotte said.

"Maybe this is too dangerous for you to pursue," Minnie said.

"I don't want Cookie hurt, but we can't let a deranged lunatic call the shots. He must be stopped." Charlotte pounded the palm of her left hand with her right fist, though it made no sound.

How could I hear ghostly footsteps yet when Charlotte made a gesture like that it was silent? I'd never understand the paranormal world.

"You said he, Charlotte; it could be she . . ." I said.

"The person who attacked you was a man, no?" Charlotte asked.

"Yes, I think so, but what if there are two people working together," I said.

Charlotte quirked an eyebrow. "Do you have two people in mind?"

"Well, there was a man and woman close to Tyler." I raised my eyebrow. "A model and her companion . . . They would definitely work together," I said.

The officer had been watching me. He'd glance over every few seconds. I tried to hide the fact that I was talking to ghosts by holding the phone up to my ear. Otherwise, the cop would have told Dylan I was crazy. I didn't want Dylan to be faced with that accusation when he would figure I had been talking with the ghosts. A few seconds later and Dylan came back out the shop's front door.

He walked over to me. "We'll need to review the video."

"Did you find anything else?" I asked.

"We're checking for fingerprints," he said.

I shook my head. "That won't help. He was wearing gloves."

"But you think it was a male?" Dylan asked.

"Based on the height and size, yes," I said. "I'll get the video for you."

"He was wearing rather large black boots too," Charlotte reminded me.

Dylan and I went to the back of the store to retrieve the video footage. Now I would be spooked every time I came back there thinking that the killer would be waiting for me. I pulled out my laptop and the video for the store.

The ghosts stood behind us. Dylan and I watched with bated breath for the image to appear. I had video for inside the shop and the outside perimeter. Movement on the video caught my attention. A person emerged from behind one of the nearby buildings. He walked with purpose toward the back of my shop. It was a spooky scene knowing what was about to happen to me. The person was dressed all in black just as I remembered. Unfortunately, there was nothing that stood out to help identify the person.

"We'll check with some other businesses to see if their surveillance caught anything," Dylan said. "I recommend keeping this back door locked."

"How did he know that the door was unlocked?" I asked.

"He obviously has been watching you," Dylan said.

"And why would he try something like this in the daytime?"

Dylan ran his hand through his hair. "Cookie, I've been trying to figure out the logic of a criminal mind for years. They can be erratic and lack common sense or rational thought."

"This I know is true," Charlotte said.

"Why do people have to be so mean?" Minnie asked around a sigh.

"That's just the way it goes sometimes, kid," Charlotte said.

"Promise me you'll keep the door locked." Dylan touched my cheek with a brush of his fingers.

I'd forgotten to lock the door when I'd brought in boxes this morning. I'd never make that mistake again. At least I hoped I never made that mistake again.

"Promise," I said.

Dylan and I watched the video again. It was no less chilling this time either. There was something odd about the person's gait. Almost as if there was a limp or an injury.

"Wait. Did you notice that?" I pointed at the screen.

I went back in the footage to replay it for Dylan.

"Did I notice what?" he asked, leaning closer to the screen.

I pointed at the person's left leg. "Notice how there's a slight pause with each step."

"Oh, I see it now," Charlotte said.

"Me too," Minnie exclaimed.

Dylan stared at the video. "That's a really good catch, Cookie. You have a keen eye."

I was shocked that I'd picked up on it since it was ever so slight. I couldn't help but smile on the inside with my discovery.

"Maybe the person has something in their shoe," Charlotte said.

"Oh, don't tell me that, Charlotte," I said.

That would mean once the item was out of the shoe the limp would be gone. There would be no way to pick the perpetrator out now.

"Who are you talking to and what did the ghost say?" Dylan asked.

I relayed the message from Charlotte.

"That's a good point, Charlotte," Dylan said.

I couldn't believe Dylan was talking to the ghosts now.

"Oh, Dylan talked to you, Charlotte. How exciting," Minnie said.

"Calm down. We don't want to get too worked up," Charlotte said.

She tried to act cool, but I knew she loved it.

"To be safe we will put an officer in the front and back of the building," Dylan said.

"Armed security? This is serious," Charlotte said.

"I'm scared," Minnie said.

I didn't like the sound of having a police officer watching the place. Though I didn't like the idea that the killer would return either. I supposed I had few other options.

"How long does this have to happen?" I asked.

"We'll just make sure that things are okay," Dylan said.

"He didn't answer the question," Charlotte said.

I suppose that was because he didn't know what to say. Now more than ever I had to find the killer. Before he found me again.

Chapter 16

Charlotte's Tips for a Fabulous Afterlife

=======================

Remember to take time for yourself.
A little relaxation goes a long way.

The rest of the day was quiet. Heather had returned in a panic. Thank goodness I'd finally gotten her to calm down. I didn't like that I had upset her, but it was better that she knew exactly what was happening. I warned her to be extra careful and aware of her surroundings. Though I guess that was good advice all the time.

I'd decided to close a little earlier than usual in light of the circumstances. Mostly I wanted to snoop around and see what Krissy and Darrin were up to. Did he have a leg injury? The ghosts were with me in the car. Along with Grandma Pearl and Tyler. I pulled the Buick away from the curb and out onto the main street. A sense of foreboding hung over town. It was probably just me trying to get over the attack.

When I checked the rearview mirror I spotted a police officer some distance behind me. That was the thing about dating a police officer. Dylan always had a friend or coworker who could help him out. Helping him in this situation meant keeping an eye on me. Of course I was grateful he cared, but I knew this officer would probably tell him what I was up to. Dylan would be upset that I was putting myself into direct danger. Was there a way I could hide my activities from the cop? I would certainly try my best.

"Can't you lose the five-o?" Charlotte asked, looking in the car's side mirror.

"If you mean trying to ditch him, no. I can't do that to Dylan," I said.

"Cookie, that's a mature and wise decision," Minnie said.

"Goody Two-shoes," Charlotte said.

I pulled up to the hotel where Darrin was staying. The VACANCY sign flashed. The parking lot was mostly empty. That was a bad thing, because I couldn't hide what I was doing. The police had asked everyone involved with the scene not to leave town until the investigation was over. That let me know that they were suspicious of Darrin and Krissy too. They had to be since they were at the scene of the crime. I pulled to the back of the hotel parking lot. The cop kept some distance, but didn't let me out of his sight. He probably wondered what I was doing here.

"Look, it's Darrin over by that car." Charlotte pointed.

Not only was Darrin out by the car, but Krissy was standing with him.

"Good catch, Charlotte," I said.

"What are they doing?" Minnie asked.

"That's what we need to find out," Charlotte said.

I pulled into a parking spot so that they wouldn't notice my car. As much as I loved my Buick, it did draw a lot of attention. The officer had stopped at the front of the hotel parking lot. Did he know this was where Darrin was staying? Probably so. Could this be a dangerous situation? I figured I was safe as long as I was in my car. I really needed to lose the cop. He was cramping my sleuthing style. I cut the engine so it wouldn't draw attention too.

"Now I wish that I could hear what they are saying," I said.

"Get out and go over there." Charlotte motioned.

"That's dangerous," Minnie said.

"The cop will see me." I peeked over my shoulder at the parked police car.

"Okay, I can take a hint. What you want is for me to find out what they are saying," Charlotte said.

"That was what I had in mind, but there's no need right now." I pointed.

Darrin and Krissy were embraced in a passionate kiss.

"Too much PDA." Charlotte stared.

"Don't watch them," I said.

"You're watching too," she said, not taking her eye off the couple.

"What is PDA?" Minnie asked.

"Public display of affection," Charlotte answered.

"Oh . . ." Minnie said through pursed lips. "That it is."

"I would say for them to get a room, but it looks as if I they already have one," Charlotte said. "They just need to use it."

After a few more seconds, they stopped kissing.

"Now what are they going to do?" Minnie asked.

The couple walked hand in hand into the room.

"It's getting late. I should go home. It's been a long day," I said.

"Well, we know she's not mad at Darrin."

"Yes, they're very much still a couple. Did they work together to kill Tyler though?" I asked.

"We have to get to the bottom of this," Charlotte said.

"Aren't you going to talk with Darrin now?" Minnie asked.

"I'd rather wait until Krissy isn't with him." I turned the ignition.

"That's probably for the best," Minnie said around a sigh.

I pulled out of the parking lot. A few seconds later, the officer was following a short distance behind me. He trailed me all the way home. I parked in the driveway and walked inside the house. Before even turning on the lights, I peeked out the window. He had parked along the street in front of the house. Was he going to stay there all night? I needed to call Dylan and ask how long I would be under guard. I'd never gotten around to replacing the door because when I told my father he'd insisted on having his friend come by and fix the door. That was probably for the best. Like Charlotte said, my thing was clothing. I wasn't that crafty with home repair. At least the handyman had been able to come by earlier in the day and replace the back door. Dylan had also insisted that I add an extra dead bolt lock to the door.

I turned on a lamp in the living room. It cast a faint yellow glow around the room. No sooner had I turned around than I spotted a piece of paper on the coffee table. Had the handyman left me a note? I reached down and picked up the piece of paper. It wasn't from the handyman.

"What's wrong, Cookie?" Charlotte asked. "You don't look so hot right now."

My hand shook as I read the paper.

You're next.

"Who left this?" My voice was barely above a whisper.

Charlotte and Minnie rushed over, peering over at the paper in my hand. We stood in stunned silence. The thought hit me. Was I alone in the house? How had the person left this note? I'd added extra locks and fixed the back door. What if this person really was still in the house? I placed the paper down on the table and inched my way back toward the kitchen. The ghosts trailed along behind me. The light in the room was still off. The faint glow from the living room lamp gave me a little bit to see by, but it wasn't much. Actually, it only added to the spookiness. The back door was shut and the glass window was still intact.

"Cookie, you have to call Dylan," Charlotte said.

"Yes, you simply must." Minnie once again stood so close that she was practically inside my body.

I had called Dylan so many times lately because of potential danger that I really didn't want to do it again.

"I know you don't want to, but you have to do it," Charlotte urged.

"As long as no one is in the house, then I don't see why I have to call," I said.

Charlotte reached for the note, but I moved it away. "This note is obviously from the killer. Dylan needs to know about it. This is part of the investigation."

I sighed. Charlotte was right. The officer was probably still in his car right out there on the street. I could just tell him, but Dylan would be upset if I did that. Plus, the cop would just call Dylan anyway.

"I should check the rest of the house first," I said.

"You're just stalling now. Dylan will come over here and look through the house." Charlotte waved her hand at me.

"Again?" I asked. "Is that really necessary?"

"Why are you asking me? Dylan's the one who will search the house. You stay here and Minnie and

I will go look through the house. In the meantime, you call Dylan." Charlotte gave me a stern look.

"Do it now," Minnie warned with a point of her finger.

Charlotte was a bad influence on Minnie. Between the two ghosts and Dylan, I knew that I was outnumbered. Besides, someone had tried to kidnap me. That was kind of a big deal. I was just being stubborn.

"Fine, I'll call him," I said.

Charlotte and Minnie disappeared around the corner. Now I was alone in the kitchen. Even though I figured no one could see in the windows, I still felt as if someone was watching me. Just my mind playing tricks on me, I suppose. Anxiety was good at doing things like that. I'd left my cell phone in my purse out in the living room.

I eased back into the living room and passed the paper on the coffee table. Of course I kept my eye on it, as if it would jump out and attack me too. I didn't even want to look over at the thing, yet I couldn't stop myself. Fear shivered down my spine. Once I reached the side table in the corner of the room I pulled my phone from my purse and hurried over to the window for a peek outside. When I inched the curtain back and peered outside, the cop car was nowhere in sight. Now he left? When I needed him?

"Nothing there," Charlotte announced.

I screamed and jumped away from the window.

The phone flew from my hand and crashed onto the floor.

"Cookie, you need to calm down. Perhaps a little herbal tea would help," Charlotte said.

Charlotte and Minnie had returned. I reached down and picked up the phone, hoping that it wasn't broken.

"Don't scare me like that," I said.

"Did you call Dylan yet?" Charlotte asked.

I touched my phone's screen and thank goodness it lit up.

I dialed his number and waited for it to ring.

"There. I did it," I said while I waited for Dylan to answer.

"Thank you," Charlotte said with a smirk.

"Hi, sweetheart," he said when he answered.

"I don't know how to tell you this." I paused.

"Just spill it," Charlotte said.

"Tell him everything." Minnie waved her arms.

It wasn't that easy. Somehow I felt responsible for this. Maybe it was because he had asked me not to get involved. Yes, that was probably it.

"I found a threatening note in my house. It was waiting for me on the coffee table. The doors are locked just as the handyman said he left them. He dropped off the keys to me earlier." My words were rushed and full of anxiety.

"I'll be there soon," Dylan said.

"I bet he's really irritated with me," I said when I clicked off the call.

"Why is that?" Minnie asked.

"Because he repeatedly has asked me not to get involved. I do the exact opposite and he has to come here and help." I plopped down on the sofa.

"Yes, that would be annoying," Charlotte said.

She wasn't exactly discouraging my behavior.

She held up her hands. "Just telling the truth."

I massaged my temples. "So you're sure you didn't notice anything unusual when you checked the rest of the house?"

"Not a thing," Charlotte said.

When a knock rattled the door I jumped again.

"If you're going to be this jumpy, then maybe you're not cut out for investigating murders," Charlotte said.

I rolled my eyes and headed for the door. As soon as I opened the door, Dylan rushed in and hugged me. I practically melted into his arms. His embrace was comforting when I needed it the most.

"Is this what you call PDA?" Minnie asked.

Charlotte howled with laughter. From over Dylan's shoulder I flashed them a disapproving glance.

"Where's the note?" he asked.

I gestured toward the living room. "I left it on the coffee table right where I found it."

He stepped into the room and walked over to the coffee table.

"That's exactly where I found it," I said. "I picked it up to read it and put it back again."

Dylan stared at the paper before pulling gloves from his pocket. Next, he took out a plastic bag.

"He comes prepared," Charlotte said.

Minnie shrugged. "I guess that's why he's the professional."

"We'll check for fingerprints right away. Unfortunately, I think it'll probably turn up nothing, just like when we tested for fingerprints on the door. This person knows what they're doing," he said, placing the note in the plastic bag.

"There were no signs of forced entry and no one is in the house. I had the door replaced and extra locks placed on the doors," I said.

"Cookie really has been investigating too much. She talks like Dylan now," Charlotte said. "No signs of forced entry?"

"Does anyone have a key?" Dylan asked.

"Just my mother and Heather," I said.

"You should give him a key," Charlotte said.

Dylan and I hadn't discussed taking our relationship to that level yet. Though I wasn't against it.

"Plus, I know they wouldn't do something like this." I pointed at the bag.

"No, of course not." Dylan released a heavy sigh. "This really is odd. I should have a look around outside."

I was at a loss too.

"I told you he would take a look around," Charlotte said.

Dylan searched every room in the house, then outside as well, but returned having found nothing out of the ordinary.

When he stepped back into the living room, he said, "Nothing odd or out of place that I can see."

"I could have told him that," Charlotte said with a wave of her hand.

"He's the expert. If something is off he would have found it," Minnie said.

"Why don't you stay at my place tonight?" Dylan asked.

"I think that's a good idea," Minnie said.

"You think I'm in danger if I stay here?" A shiver ran down my spine.

"It's just that I know you'll worry and not get any sleep," Dylan said.

"Cookie's a creature of habit. She doesn't like sleeping anywhere other than her own bed," Charlotte said.

I would argue with Charlotte, but she was right.

"Would you want to stay here?" I asked.

Dylan smiled. "Sure, I can stay with you."

Though I didn't look at Charlotte, I knew she had a smile plastered on her face. I knew that the slightest noise would spook me. Dylan had his own place though. I couldn't have him stay over every night. Though Charlotte would love that idea. She already had my wedding planned and I hadn't even been asked.

Chapter 17

Cookie's Savvy Tips for Vintage Clothing Shopping

*Wearing vintage can add a little fun or glamour.
You don't have to reserve wearing vintage for
going out of the house. Try nightgowns,
robes, or pajamas for a little vintage flair.*

The next morning, I made a little stop on my way to the shop. Dylan had left early. I'd made breakfast of pancakes with blueberry syrup. Nothing like starting off the day with a little comfort food. That didn't mean I didn't have a police escort though. Another officer from the Sugar Creek Police Department had followed me. I wasn't complaining now. Not after finding the note in my house. I had surveillance cameras for the shop, but I decided I needed to add them to my home as well.

When I pulled into the hotel parking lot, I wasn't sure what I was looking for, but I had to know what Krissy and her boyfriend were up to. Since I hadn't talked to them last night when I stopped here, I thought this morning might be different. Receiving that note had made me more determined than ever to find the killer.

"Exactly what do you think you'll discover by sitting here?" Charlotte asked.

"I don't know, but I find their relationship to be odd." I stared at the hotel room door where they had entered last night.

"It's not the relationship that's odd, they're odd. Two odd people together make for an odd everything," Charlotte said. "They are odd separately though. Add them together and it's madness."

"That's a lot of odd," Minnie said with a laugh.

"You can't sit here all day," Charlotte said.

"I think they'll come out for breakfast soon," I said, not taking my eyes off the door.

"Maybe they'll order room service," Charlotte said.

"They don't have room service here. Unless you count the vending machines around the corner," I said as I tapped my fingers against the steering wheel.

"Oh, here they come." Minnie thrust her arm forward from the backseat, pointing.

"Where?" I asked.

"I don't see them," Charlotte said.

Minnie sighed. "Sorry, that was just the tree branch moving with the wind."

Minnie was a bit excited. Movement from the right caught my attention. It wasn't the couple, but someone else was behind one of the tall shrubs next to the building. She had shoulder-length brown hair. It seemed strange though, almost as if it was a wig.

"What in the world is that woman doing?" Charlotte asked.

"She's acting odd, isn't she?" I asked.

"You could say that, yes." Charlotte leaned forward in the front seat as if that would give her a better view.

After staring for a bit longer I recognized the woman.

"Do you know who that is?" I asked with excitement in my voice.

"As a matter of fact, I do know who she is. What is she doing here?" Charlotte asked.

"Who is it? I can't see that well from back here." Minnie leaned forward, placing her forearms on the back of the seat. "Plus, I don't know as many people as you two."

Shanna Sizemore was sneaking around the hotel. Why was she trying to hide?

"There is definitely something fishy going on here," Charlotte said. "You should get to the bottom of it."

"This can't be a coincidence. Do you think I should confront her?" I asked.

Charlotte looked at me. "Yes, I think you should ask her just exactly what she thinks she's doing."

Though this made me a bit nervous, I opened the car door and headed across the parking lot. Checking over my shoulder, I wanted to see if the police officer was still parked there and watching me. He was still there. How much trouble could I get into with the cop watching me? Knowing my luck . . . plenty of trouble. The ghosts walked with me as we neared the area where Shanna was hiding. She still hadn't noticed that I was approaching her. That changed quickly though.

Shanna peered up and our eyes locked on each other. For a second she was frozen. Her shocked expression and the terror in her eyes caught me off guard. Without saying a word she jumped up and took off around the side of the building. I ran after her, but when I reached the edge of the building she was already out of sight.

"She sure does run fast," Charlotte said.

I peered around to see if I could spot her. She was nowhere in sight. I tried to catch my breath.

The officer ran up behind me. "Cookie, are you all right?"

This was a little embarrassing. I was used to doing crazy things with only the ghosts watching.

"I'm fine," I said, forcing a smile.

Though now I had to give him an explanation for why I'd been running and was out of breath.

"I saw a suspicious-looking woman hiding in the bushes. So I decided to find out what she was up to."

"You should wait in the car just to be safe. I'll have a look around for her. What does she look like?" he asked.

She'd probably taken the wig off by now.

"Average height with brown hair . . . maybe," I said. He frowned.

"I think she was wearing a wig," I added.

He nodded. "Okay, wait for me, please."

"He's wasting his time. She's long gone," Charlotte said with a wave of her hand.

Heading back to the Buick with the ghosts, we climbed in and waited for the officer to return. I hated sitting there and doing nothing. I felt as if I could be searching for Shanna. Plus, I still hadn't gotten around to talking with Darrin.

I tapped my fingers against the steering wheel again.

"Will you stop that? You're giving me a panic attack," Charlotte said.

"It is a little distracting," Minnie added.

She caught me watching her through the rearview mirror. I suppose tension was high and anxiety was spiked.

"I just can't get rid of my anxiety," I said.

Another minute passed and the officer walked back to my car.

"No sign of her. Are you sure you saw someone?" he asked.

"If he'd been paying attention he would have seen her too," Charlotte said.

"I'm positive," I said.

"It's probably best if you see something like that to come and get me first. Under the circumstances it's a bit dangerous for you," he said.

"The officer is right, Cookie," Minnie said.

"Cookie can handle herself," Charlotte said.

I forced a smile. "I'll make sure and do that."

I knew he was helping me, but I was stubborn.

"I'll go to work now," I said.

He smiled. "I'll follow you."

"We know you will," Charlotte said.

After pulling out of the parking lot, I drove the rest of the way to the shop. Now I had to find Shanna and ask her why she was snooping around the hotel. People were blissfully unaware of the potential danger that loomed as they strolled along the sidewalks and drove up and down the streets of Sugar Creek. If I could help it they would stay that way too. I wouldn't allow a murderer to walk free. Not if there was any way possible for me to solve the crime. When I pulled up to the shop, I spotted Ken heading down the sidewalk. His office was on the opposite side of town. Not that it was far, though, since Sugar Creek was such a small town.

"He's here to see you early," Charlotte said.

I rolled the Buick up to the curb in front of the shop and cut the engine. "I hope nothing's wrong."

"Well, hurry up. I'm curious to find out what he wants." Charlotte motioned for me to get moving.

"More like you are nosy and want to know why he's here."

Charlotte gasped as I got out of the car.

"Cookie Chanel, you are too sassy for your own good." Charlotte rushed behind me.

"Pot meet kettle," I said.

Minnie laughed from over my shoulder. Grandma Pearl meowed as she and Tyler rushed down the sidewalk ahead of us. People in town probably thought I was officially a crazy cat lady. I hurried down the sidewalk. Just as I was about to call out to Ken, I realized he wasn't stopping at my front door. He walked by my shop and over to Heather's.

"He didn't even notice you," Charlotte said in a stunned voice.

Ken paused until Heather opened the door for him. He walked inside. They never looked over and noticed that I had been watching them. Charlotte and I exchanged a look.

"Something weird is going on with those two," Charlotte said.

"Should I go over and check or mind my own business?" I asked.

Now who was the nosy one? I should definitely mind my own business.

"Maybe they're planning a surprise birthday party for you, after all," Minnie said.

"I doubt they'd be doing that this early," I said. "I suppose it's none of my business. If they're in trouble they'll come to me."

I stepped in front of my shop and unlocked the door.

"Just one little peek in the window wouldn't hurt," Charlotte said, trying to persuade me.

"If you want a peek you can go over there." I opened the shop door.

Wind Song rushed past me and into the shop. I knew it was Wind Song in control because the cat made a beeline for the counter where I kept the food. Grandma Pearl was just holding on for the ride at this point. Tyler wasn't quite so quick to make it to the food dish. As grouchy as he was, the cat he was sharing bodies with probably didn't want to complain.

I figured if I told Charlotte to go she would understand that it was wrong to invade their privacy and not go over to Heather's place. I was wrong. After all this time I should have known Charlotte better than that. Charlotte left my side and was now in front of Heather's shop. I hoped she only looked in the window and didn't actually go inside.

Minnie stayed with me.

"Now I have to go after her," I said.

"I'll go with you," Minnie said.

Minnie and I marched over to Heather's shop. I stopped at the door. I spotted Charlotte through the window, but didn't see Heather or Ken.

"Charlotte," I whispered as if someone would overhear me.

I was the only one at this section of the sidewalk. Though the cop was parked just down the street. I hoped he didn't see me. That would only add to his thought that I was a bit bonkers. I could only imagine what he would tell Dylan. A few more seconds passed and Charlotte returned. She stared at me, but didn't say anything.

"Well, what are they doing?" I asked.

"Oh, now you want to know," she said, inspecting her plum-color-painted fingernails. Charlotte changed her outfits and nail color quite often.

"It doesn't matter," I said with a wave of my hand.

Charlotte picked imaginary lint off her black trousers. "Maybe I shouldn't tell you."

I turned and rushed back toward the shop. "Fine. I don't want to know anyway."

Charlotte and Minnie hurried after me.

"Okay, if you must know," Charlotte said. "They're just talking."

I flipped on the light switch and stuffed my purse under the counter. "I'm surprised you didn't stay around to find out what they were talking about."

I poured food into the cat dish. Wind Song narrowed her bright green eyes at me. She wasn't happy that I'd made her wait.

Charlotte waved her hand. "It was probably boring. You want to know though, don't you?"

I picked up a shirt and folded it. "Like I said, I don't care."

Charlotte opened her mouth to say something else, but the door opening caught her attention. A customer walked in. Her focus was set on me as she crossed the room. The woman was tall with long brown hair. Her smile lit up the room.

"Good morning. Welcome to It's Vintage Y'all," I said. "May I help you?"

"Just looking around," the woman said, turning to the right.

That was odd. I'd thought for sure she was coming to talk to me. She walked toward the rack of dresses that lined the far right wall.

"She looks familiar," Minnie said.

"Yes, I've seen her before too." Charlotte moved closer to the customer.

I studied the woman and realized that I'd also seen her before. I jotted down a note and showed it to Charlotte and Minnie.

"That's where we've seen her. She was one of the models at the photo shoot," Charlotte said.

The woman must have sensed me staring. She looked up and smiled once again. Why would she be here?

"That doesn't seem like a coincidence," Charlotte said.

I agreed and this meant that I needed to ask her what she was doing here. Well, I wouldn't come right out and say that, but I would get around to the point. I moved from around the corner and over to the woman.

When I got close I pulled out a turquoise and yellow Emilio Pucci dress. "This would look amazing on you."

"What are you talking about, Cookie? Everything in this store would look amazing on her. Look at her long legs, gorgeous eyes, dazzling hair, and perfect complexion," Charlotte said.

That was true, but this was a way for me to break the ice. By the way the woman looked at me, I figured she knew what I was doing. Had she come here specially to speak with me about Tyler? How did she know I was involved with the investigation? I was probably putting too much thought into it. She was probably just here to look at the vintage

clothing. No, my instincts had to be correct. I'd
push for more information.

The model eyed the dress. "It's lovely."

"Don't mess this up, Cookie. Get her to talk,"
Charlotte said.

The model watched me. It was as if she wanted to
say something, but didn't know how to start the
conversation. That meant I'd have to do it for her.

"I know you, right? You were one of the models
for the photo shoot?" I asked.

"I'm so nervous," Minnie said.

"Cookie, you can handle this. Get her to talk,"
Charlotte said.

It was as if I had my own paranormal cheerleaders.

The model nodded.

As she remained tight-lipped I pushed for more
conversation. "How are you?"

"I'm doing well," she said as she studied another
blouse.

"This is going to be painful if we keep going at
this pace," Charlotte said around a sigh.

I was quickly tiring of my cheerleaders. The
model wasn't making this easy.

"Have you heard anything about if they found
the killer?" I asked.

"I doubt she believes your clueless act," Charlotte
said around a sigh.

The model picked up a black and white Lorrie
Deb linen short-sleeved dress. "I haven't heard
anything. I'm just still in shock that it happened."

"Okay, this is a start. I was beginning to think she'd forgotten how to talk," Charlotte said.

"She must be scared," Minnie said.

"Did you see anything unusual that day?" I asked.

She placed the dress back on the rack. "No, I suppose I didn't."

I wouldn't let the conversation stop there. Not if I could help it.

"Did Tyler act any differently?"

"He was just being his usual self," she said with a wave of her hand.

"And what was that like? I didn't know him well." I studied her face for a reaction.

Of course I knew he was cranky and demanding, but I wanted to hear her impression.

"She will probably wonder why you're asking so many questions," Charlotte said. "Just don't let her get away without more answers."

"Tyler was always hitting on all the models. That gave him a reputation, of course. It was a bit stressful working for him sometimes."

"I'd say so. She should have let the jerk have it." Charlotte pumped her fist.

"Maybe she did," Minnie said with a raised eyebrow.

"Good point, Minnie." Charlotte eyed the woman up and down.

"What did he do to you?" I asked.

"He was always asking me and the other models

out on dates. Needless to say that made his girlfriend extremely mad."

"I guess that's why she broke up with him," I said.

"You'd think so, wouldn't you? I don't think that was the case. He broke up with her. I think she was crazier than he was, and that's saying a lot," she said.

Tyler hissed from his spot in the corner of the room. She looked in his direction.

"Sounds like Tyler and his girlfriend were a match made in heaven. They should have stayed together," Charlotte said.

"Plus, Tyler owed Krissy money. She was another one of the models there that day," the model said.

"Oh, we're well aware of who she is," Charlotte said with a sarcastic look.

"Why did he owe her money?" I asked.

"I think he liked to gamble," she said.

"That would certainly give Krissy a reason to murder Tyler," Charlotte said.

"Did he ask you for money?" I asked.

She scoffed. "It wouldn't have done him any good. I don't have extra money to lend."

"I understand that," I said.

The model sorted through the rack of clothing. "You know, I think someone has been following me."

Charlotte moved closer. "Whoa, now this is getting interesting."

I frowned. "Who has been following you? Why do you think someone is following you?"

"She could have a stalker," Charlotte suggested.

"I've never actually seen anyone, but I've noticed strange things at my place."

"This is odd," Charlotte said.

"What kind of strange things?" I asked.

"Things have been moved at the hotel room, and I hear noises at night as if someone is trying to break in," she said.

"That sounds like what has been happening to you," Minnie said.

"It does sound like the same stuff," Charlotte said. "I doubt this is a coincidence."

"Have you told the police about this?" I asked.

"She should tell the police," Charlotte said.

"No, I wasn't sure there was anything really to tell. I have no proof."

Now I was worried about her safety. What if the killer came for her next?

"You really should let them know. Just to be safe. If it's nothing, then there's no harm done," I said.

"I'll think about it," she said. "Well, I've taken up enough of your time."

"Let me know if anything else happens?" I grabbed my card from the counter and handed it to her.

She took the card. "Yes, I will call you."

"Isn't she going to buy anything?" Charlotte asked in a disappointed voice.

Charlotte always wanted to sell. Forever the businesswoman.

The model walked out the door. I followed her to the window. I peered out, watching her walk away down the sidewalk. A woman stepped out from behind a nearby building. Unfortunately, I couldn't make out any features or get a description of the woman. She wore a blue baseball cap and dark sunglasses. She fell into step directly behind the model. There was something strange about the way she walked. Even though I couldn't see what the woman's face looked like, I was sure I recognized her.

"Hey, isn't that Shanna?" Charlotte pointed.

"It is her!" Minnie said.

Grandma Pearl meowed and pawed at the window.

"What is she doing following that model too?" I asked.

"This is strange," Charlotte said.

I wanted to follow and see just how far Shanna trailed the woman, but I couldn't leave the shop. What if Shanna wanted to harm the woman? Was she the one who had been doing the strange things? Why though? Her only connection with Tyler was that they'd talked and were supposed to meet. That was hardly a reason for murder. Though I suppose people had murdered for a lot less.

"There's something more to this story," Charlotte said, as if she'd read my mind.

I pulled out my phone.

"Who are you calling?" Charlotte asked.

"I think I need to tell Dylan about Shanna's strange behavior."

"That's a good idea," Minnie said.

Dylan picked up right away. "Cookie, are you okay?"

His voice was full of alarm. All my snooping around had caused him to be panicked every time I called him. That wasn't good. I explained what had happened.

"Thank you, Dylan," I said.

"I'll stop by soon," Dylan said.

When I ended the call, Charlotte asked, "Well, what did he say?"

"Dylan said he would have the officer follow them. If he sees Shanna he'll stop her and ask why she's following the woman."

Chapter 18

Charlotte's Tips for a Fabulous Afterlife
========

Did I mention you have to nag the living?
That can be exhausting.
Hence my previous tip for why relaxation is important.

I stood by the window for a bit longer. Now the police officer had left the front of my store. What if the killer took this time to slip back in? I knew I had locked the back door, but maybe I should check once again. No, that would be excessive. I was letting my mind work overtime with crazy thoughts.

"You have to find out what this Shanna woman is up to." Charlotte leaned against the counter. "How many people is she following?"

"I will send her another message," I said, pulling out my phone.

"It's doubtful she will speak with you since she thinks you stood her up at the diner," Charlotte said.

"She probably hates Cash now," Minnie said.

"Who?" Charlotte asked with a frown.

"That was the fake man's name." Minnie waved her hand.

"Oh right, right," Charlotte said.

"I have no other way to get in touch with Shanna," I said.

Charlotte sighed. "I suppose you can give it a try."

"It can't hurt, right?" Minnie asked.

Charlotte raised an eyebrow. "Don't be so sure."

I typed in a message on the app to Shanna.

Sorry I missed you the other day. Something came up. I tried to message you, but I figured it was too late and you were mad at me. I can't stop thinking about you though. Can we meet? I promise to be there this time.

When I finished, I set the phone on the counter.

"Oh, you are way more devious than I ever thought," Charlotte said with pleasure in her voice.

"No, I'm not. I don't like doing that at all, but it had to be done." I blew out a deep breath.

We stared at the phone, as if she would respond immediately.

"What are we doing? If she responds at all it could be hours," I said.

"Maybe even never," Minnie said.

"Maybe even never," Charlotte said in her usual dry tone, mocking Minnie.

"Oh, Charlotte, stop being so negative," I said.

"Me negative? She's the one who said Shanna may never respond." Charlotte scowled.

Again, we watched the phone. Still nothing happened. This was a waste of time.

"I wish she would answer," Minnie said.

When the bell over the door jingled we all jumped. Charlotte and Minnie screeched.

Heather chuckled. "What are you all staring at?"

I sighed. "It's a long story."

"I have time," Heather said as she walked across the room.

"I don't know if I've ever seen you with this much bounce in your step." Charlotte eyed Heather.

Heather blushed. "What? I'm always happy."

"Something's going on with her," Charlotte said, gesturing toward Heather.

"There's nothing going on with me." Heather looked down when she answered. "Just being my usual happy self. Nothing wrong with that."

Heather staring at her feet while she talked was a sure sign that something was definitely going on with her. I guessed by the smile that it was something good.

"Are you going to tell us what it is?" I asked, tapping my fingers on the countertop.

Heather touched the bangle bracelets on display at the end of the counter. "Like I said, it's nothing."

Charlotte and I exchanged a look. I'd get Heather to lay it all out sooner or later. In the meantime I filled Heather in on what had just happened.

Heather looked down at my phone. "Look, she answered."

Charlotte reached for the phone, but her hand went straight through.

"Nice try," Heather said.

"You can't blame a girl for trying," Charlotte said.

I grabbed the phone. Minnie and Charlotte hurried over and peered over my shoulder.

"What does she say?" Minnie asked.

"She wants to meet." I looked up at the three staring faces.

Actually make that five staring faces. Grandma Pearl and Tyler had moved over to the counter now.

"Well, isn't that what you wanted?" Heather asked.

"Yes, I'm just surprised and a little nervous."

"I can go with you," Heather said.

"Would you? I would appreciate that," I said.

"Just tell me when and where." Heather smiled.

"She said we can meet at the park."

Tyler meowed. Did he want to use the board to talk? I'd have to ask soon.

"Well, at least it's a public place," Charlotte said.

"Let me know when you're going to meet up with her. I should get back to my shop. I have an appointment soon." Heather gestured over her shoulder.

Her face lit up when she mentioned her appointment. That hadn't gone unnoticed by me.

Charlotte held her hand up. "Not so fast."

Heather turned around to face Charlotte. "What's wrong, Charlotte?"

"You still haven't told us why you're so happy."

Charlotte narrowed her eyes and placed her hands on her hips.

Minnie and I stared at Heather, waiting for a response.

"Can't a girl just be happy for no reason?" Heather asked with a shrug of her shoulders.

"No," Charlotte said matter-of-factly.

Heather placed her hands on her hips. "What is wrong with y'all?"

"Heather, I'm your best friend. You know you can tell me everything. My feelings will be hurt if you're keeping secrets from me," I said.

"I think she is keeping secrets. She's acting funny. Not to mention the weird sightings with Ken," Charlotte said.

Heather sighed. "You're right, Cookie, I shouldn't keep secrets from you."

Now Charlotte, Minnie, and I stood in front of Heather.

"You can tell us anything," we said in unison.

"It's just that I didn't know how you would feel about it." Heather looked down at her shoes again.

"I'm sure whatever you say I will be happy if you're happy," I said.

"Okay, here goes. It's just that Ken has been coming over for readings and I think we have a lot in common. I kind of like him." Heather once more stared at her shoes.

Her cheeks were completely red now. I'd never seen her this way.

"I knew it," Charlotte said.

I suppose the signs were there. I should have guessed from the beginning. Why hadn't I realized that they would be a perfect match for each other? Okay, maybe they were opposites, but opposites attract. My mother and father's love story was a great example of opposites . . . and they were celebrating their fortieth anniversary soon.

I moved around the counter and wrapped my arms around Heather. "I think this is a wonderful thing."

Heather looked at me. "Are you sure?"

I nodded. "Ken is a great guy. He would be lucky to get someone as fantastic as you."

Heather smiled again. "Well, I don't know for sure if he likes me back."

"I doubt he's coming around for your readings." Charlotte scoffed.

Heather ignored Charlotte's comment. "I'm glad that I got that off my chest. I really need to go, but we'll talk later?"

I hugged her again. "Sure, we'll talk later."

Heather walked out of the shop with a bounce in her step.

"Wow, Heather and Ken. I never would have thought they would be a match. Opposites attract though," Charlotte said.

"That's exactly what I thought, Charlotte," I said.

"How do you feel about that?" Charlotte asked with a raised eyebrow.

"I think it's great," I said with a wave of my hand. "I just want Heather and Ken to be happy."

I felt Charlotte's stare on me. "Are you sure about that?"

"Of course she's sure," Minnie said.

"I mean, it's obvious Ken and I weren't meant for each other." I busied myself folding a shirt. "I want her to find someone to love."

Charlotte continued eyeing me as if that would force me to talk. There was nothing else to say on the subject.

After another minute of being watched, I said, "I'm happy . . . really."

Charlotte shrugged. "If you say so."

While I waited for the time to meet Shanna I wanted to look into a couple things. One, I needed to ask Krissy about that gambling debt Tyler supposedly owed her. Two, I wanted to find out more about Tyler's girlfriend, Tina. Though I had almost convinced myself that Shanna was somehow involved in the murder. Why she would do this, I wasn't sure. She barely knew Tyler, so why would she want to kill him? Perhaps he had stood her up as well. Oh dear. What if she tried to kill me at the park? If she ever figured out I was the person behind the fake dating profile, I would be a goner. After all, it wasn't nice to toy with people's emotions.

"I think I did a very bad thing," I said as I placed an Issey Miyake rolled-neck blouse onto a hanger.

"Oh no, what have you done now?" Charlotte asked.

"I shouldn't have tricked Shanna like that. It wasn't a nice thing to do," I said.

Charlotte rubbed her temples. "Oh, here we go again. Cookie, I explained this to you. Yes, it is bad that you had to do this, but it was completely necessary. You aren't doing it because you get a kick out of it." She frowned. "You don't get a kick out of it, right?"

"No, of course not." I placed my hands on my hips.

"All right. You want to solve this case and sometimes you have to do sneaky things. Shanna will get over it."

"Will she? What if Tyler stood her up and she killed him because of it?" I placed the folded shirt on the display table in the center of the room.

Charlotte quirked an eyebrow. "Honestly, she's obviously unhinged if something like that would drive her to kill. There are a lot of things that would probably drive her over the edge."

I nodded. "I suppose you're right."

"Of course I'm right, darling. Charlotte is always right." She winked.

"I wouldn't go so far as to say that," I said.

She scowled. "Just be glad that you have me to talk some sense into you once in a while."

"Shanna won't really come 'unhinged,' will she?" Minnie used air quotes. "If so, I definitely have to do something about this."

Charlotte eyed Minnie. "We never know who might come unhinged. Cookie might come unhinged for all we know."

I placed my hands on my hips. "What? I will not come unhinged, for heaven's sake."

"Well, you do talk to ghosts . . . just sayin' . . ." Charlotte waved her hand.

"Oh! Stop it, Charlotte." I pulled out my phone.

"What are you doing now?" Charlotte asked. "Don't tell me you want to cancel the meeting with Shanna after all that we just talked about." Charlotte reached for my phone, but as usual her hand went right through.

I moved my phone anyway in case next time she tried it actually worked. "When are you going to stop trying that? I'm not canceling. I just want to find out more information about Tyler's ex-girlfriend."

"How do you plan to do that?" Minnie asked.

"I need to make a few calls about her," I said.

"That means she has no idea what she's doing," Charlotte said.

"I do have an idea, smarty-pants." I smirked.

"Okay, Cookie Chanel, let's hear it." Charlotte placed her hands on her hips.

She'd used my first and last name. That meant she was irritated with me. After typing into my laptop for a few seconds I discovered what I was searching for.

"Aha. I found the ex-girlfriend's number. I'm going to call her," I said with a smile.

"Oh dear, this will not end well," Charlotte said.

"We'll see about that." I dialed the number.

Charlotte and Minnie stared at me as I listened to the rings on the other end of the line.

"Put the call on speaker." Charlotte pointed at the phone.

"Yes, I want to hear," Minnie said.

I quirked an eyebrow. "Only if you're nice."

Charlotte narrowed her eyes. "You seem to forget that I like to sing at night."

Ugh. She had me there. I didn't want to listen to her off-key, late-night karaoke. Her rendition of that eighties song "Puttin' on the Ritz" was pure torture. Of course for the rest of the day the song was stuck in my head. As soon as I put it on speakerphone a woman answered. It was odd that her voice sounded familiar. Though I knew we'd never spoken before.

"She sounds scary," Minnie said.

"Maybe you caught her in the middle of something," Charlotte said.

"Good afternoon. Is this Tina Fairchild?" I asked.

"Who wants to know?" the woman asked in a harsh tone.

"Now she's just being rude," Charlotte said. "Oh, I bet she thinks you're a telemarketer. That causes some people to snap."

"My name is Cookie Chanel."

Silence filled the line. A couple seconds passed.

"Hello?" I called out.

There was no answer. When I checked the phone sitting on the counter I realized the call had been dropped.

"Do you think she hung up on purpose or was the call dropped?" I asked.

"Probably on purpose. Something seems off about her. I don't know what happened to the call, but you should call her back," Charlotte said.

I dialed the number again, but it rang several times until finally going to her voice mail. I decided to leave a message: "Tina, this is Cookie Chanel calling you back. It's important that I speak with you. If you could call me back as soon as possible that would be great."

After leaving the message, I clicked off the call.

"The fact that she didn't answer this time probably means she ended the call on purpose," Charlotte said.

"Not necessarily," I said. "Maybe she's in an area that has bad cell phone coverage."

Charlotte scoffed. "I suppose."

I knew Charlotte was suspicious. I was suspicious too. If Tina didn't call me back I would try her

again. In the meantime, I wanted to know more
about her.

"I think I need to do a little research," I said.

"Good luck with that," Charlotte said.

"I have my ways," I said with a smile.

Chapter 19

Cookie's Savvy Tips for Vintage Clothing Shopping
=====

Don't forget to look for wardrobe essentials.
Things like simple blouses, sweaters, blazers, and slacks.

I turned the CLOSED sign around on the shop door, leaving the cats inside, hoping I wouldn't be gone too long. Before going to the park to meet with Shanna, I headed back to the bed-and-breakfast where Krissy was staying to track her down. I wasn't going to let her get away without talking to me this time. I pulled into the driveway and cut the engine. Before even getting out of the car I spotted movement out of the corner of my eye. Krissy was walking around the side of the house. Darrin was following close behind her.

I hurried and unfastened my seat belt. "I'm not letting them get away from me this time."

"Why do they always look as if they are arguing?" Minnie asked.

"Because they are always arguing," Charlotte answered.

I jumped out of the car and rushed toward the house.

"Be careful, Cookie," Minnie said.

"I don't think you should let them know you're here if they're fighting," Charlotte said as she followed me.

As we suspected, the sound of raised voices carried around the corner, which must mean they were in another argument. Their fighting was exhausting. I stopped short at the edge of the house, hiding behind the azalea bush. They were clearly mad at each other.

"I wanted to get my money back from him, and you ruined it," Krissy said.

Charlotte and I exchanged a look. By *ruined it*, did Krissy mean that Darrin had killed Tyler?

"I did the best that I could. You are always blaming me when things go wrong," Darrin said.

I needed to get him to admit that he had killed Tyler. So far, they were only hinting that they had done something to Tyler.

"I didn't ask you to come here anyway," Krissy said.

"Oh please. You would have called me crying that you missed me less than twenty-four hours after getting here. I saved us all time by coming before you had a chance to complain. You complain if I come with you and complain if I don't." Darrin's voice was full of anger.

"Oh, there really is trouble in paradise," Charlotte said.

"I feel bad listening to them argue. It makes me uncomfortable," Minnie said.

I stood there with my back pressed against the

brick wall, straining to hear every word. Now they had stopped talking though.

"What are they doing?" Charlotte asked. "Do you think they've killed each other?"

"With the way they were fighting that's entirely possible," Minnie said.

Only about two seconds had passed when the nightmare scenario occurred. Krissy and Darrin came around the corner. There was no time for me to get away. They looked right at me, stopping in their tracks.

"What are you doing?" Krissy asked.

Darrin's face turned even redder. It looked as if he wanted to snap me in two like a twig. I wanted to confront Krissy and Darrin with what I'd heard, but I also realized that they could be involved in Tyler's murder. Maybe it was best if I ran for my car.

Krissy moved closer to me. "You are always snooping around. I think it's time you learned to mind your own business."

"Oh, Cookie, this is bad. You should run now," Minnie said.

"Don't let them see your fear. It will only make things worse. Act tough." Charlotte pumped her fist.

Should I stand my ground and act tough like Charlotte suggested? Or to the car like Minnie advised? For my safety I decided to take Minnie's advice and run for the car. I sprinted away from the house and jumped into the Buick. I cranked the engine. Krissy and Darrin stood at the edge of the house. They were glaring at me.

"Well, that was a pathetic display," Charlotte said.

"I did what was best for my own good. The cop couldn't come help me if he didn't know I was in danger." I navigated a left turn.

"I think you did the right thing, Cookie," Minnie said.

I swung by the shop and picked up the cats. All I wanted to do now was head home and have a bowl of cookies 'n' cream ice cream. The entire ride home I was on guard. Would Krissy and Darrin follow me? Now that I was home I plopped down on the sofa. My phone alerted me to a message on the dating app. Now the adrenaline was really pumping. Oh no, I had forgotten about the park!

"I got a message from Shanna," I said.

Charlotte and Minnie rushed over. They'd been standing in the corner of the room whispering. They did a lot of that lately.

"Well, what does it say?" Charlotte asked.

I clicked on the app and read the message. "She said for me to take a leap off a short pier."

Charlotte laughed.

I gave her a warning scowl.

"Sorry, but that is funny," she said around another laugh.

So now I wasn't going to meet Shanna. I'd have to think of another plan. Lately my sleuthing skills had been lacking.

Chapter 20

Charlotte's Tips for a Fabulous Afterlife
═══════════════
Don't let the living get too testy.

"Why did I wait until it was almost dark to come to a cemetery?" I whispered as I opened the gate and stepped inside.

The hinges groaned as they moved with the motion. At least I hoped that was where the noise had come from. The sound also resembled that of a ghost moaning.

"You lack any self-control and had to come as soon as the thought hit you?" Charlotte answered.

I cast a salty look her way. "Thank you. Perhaps it's because I have a pesky ghost following me around and she always insists I do things and pretends as if she never did such a thing."

Charlotte lifted an eyebrow. "That doesn't sound accurate to me."

"Am I a pesky ghost?" Minnie asked as she followed me into the graveyard.

"No, not you, Minnie." I looked at Charlotte again.

"I can't believe you wore that to snoop around in a graveyard." Charlotte eyed me up and down.

"If I'd known I was coming maybe I wouldn't have worn this," I said.

"It's a lovely outfit," Minnie said.

Maybe my choice of a white pleated skirt with multi-colored flecks in the pattern wasn't the best idea. The skirt fell to just above my knees. My black top was Jean-Louis Scherrer with button fastenings at the shoulders.

The wind picked up and the tree branches swayed. Dark clouds were moving in quickly. It would storm soon. The sound of the rustling branches added a creepy sound effect. What was I scared for anyway? I already had ghosts following me. Not to mention two cats with spirits of humans stuck inside.

There could be bad spirits around though. The last thing I wanted was to encounter those. Plus, there had been a murder here. What were the odds that the killer would ever return though? I had nothing to worry about, I reminded myself. So why were my knees still shaking?

"What are we looking for?" Minnie asked.

"Ask Charlotte. It was her idea to come here," I said.

"It was not my idea. Besides, you agreed to it quickly," Charlotte said.

"So it was your idea," I said.

Charlotte waved her hand. "Never mind that. We should head over to the scene of the crime."

The ghosts, cats, and I weaved around the old headstones toward the back of the graveyard. The sound of movement caught my attention. I whipped around to see who was behind me. No one was there. Not that I could see anyway. Another ghost? My legs shook so badly that it was hard to walk.

"Did you see anything?" I whispered.

Charlotte and Minnie were huddled together. They shook their heads. The cats were together and right behind the ghosts. Talk about scaredy-cats. I turned back around to continue toward the back of the graveyard. A whisper of a cool breeze carried across my skin. It was still hot out. How had the air been cold? I reached the spot where Tyler had been murdered. He stood by my feet. When I looked down at him he meowed.

"I know you don't like it here, but we're trying to figure out who murdered you," I said.

"Yes, this is a necessary trip," Charlotte added.

Grandma Pearl placed her paw on Tyler's.

"That is so sweet," Minnie said.

"So do you think someone could have been hiding nearby? Maybe it wasn't anyone who was at the photo shoot," I said, looking around the grave-yard. "The person was waiting for him to get in a spot that was less noticeable."

"By someone do you mean Shanna?" Charlotte quirked an eyebrow.

"I suppose. She could have lured him to this spot," I said.

"That sounds like something she would do," Minnie said.

The sun was setting and it was quickly growing dark around us.

"What about over there?" I pointed.

"The mausoleum?" Charlotte asked.

"Yes, that would be a good place to hide."

"I suppose it would be a good place to hide," Charlotte said. "It's creepy just like Shanna."

Everyone followed as I walked around the gravestones over to the concrete structure. Vines of ivy grew up the side with moss covering much of the stone.

I walked behind it. "The person could have been hiding over here. When they saw Tyler over there talking on his phone the person ran out. Once they'd killed him, I imagine they ran back here."

"Where did the person go?" Charlotte asked.

I peered around. There were trees close by. "I guess they ran over to the trees and hid behind them until they could reach the fence. Next they climbed the fence and disappeared from sight."

"Or they could have hidden inside the mausoleum until the coast was clear," Charlotte said.

"I feel like they would have been caught that way."

"Yes, but what if the police never thought to check in there?" Charlotte raised an eyebrow.

"I guess they could have missed that," I said.

"See, I have good ideas." Charlotte smiled.

"I'll have to ask Dylan if he looked in there. Though it'll be tough to explain why I'm asking." I walked around to the entrance of the mausoleum.

The door had iron bars with an intricate scroll design covering the front.

"Well, what are you waiting for?" Charlotte pointed.

"I don't think this is such a good idea." Minnie was hiding behind Charlotte.

After releasing a deep breath, I reached out and grabbed the handle of the iron door cover. A loud groan echoed eerily as I opened the door.

"That was spooky," Minnie said, rubbing her arms to fight off the imagined chill.

"What are you doing?" Charlotte asked.

"Checking to see if the door is unlocked. If it's locked we know the person couldn't have hidden inside here," I said.

"Cookie, don't you dare go in there," Charlotte ordered. "I'm putting my foot down."

"Why would I do something like that? I'm not actually going inside this thing," I said.

"Because you do crazy things sometimes, that's why," she said. "I don't know if I can trust you to behave."

"Don't worry. Everything is fine," I said, dismissing her comment. "And if anyone misbehaves, it's you."

She narrowed her eyes at me as if she didn't believe a word I said. I reached for the door behind the iron one. When I pushed it slowly opened. The damp earth smell overwhelmed my nostrils. Of course the space was dark.

"Cookie," Charlotte whispered.

"What is it, Charlotte?" I asked.

Charlotte pointed. "I thought I saw a person over there by the trees."

I looked in the direction of her pointing finger. I saw nothing out of the ordinary.

"I see nothing out of place, Charlotte."

"I think you should go check it out," Charlotte said.

"We'll go with you," Minnie added.

I suppose it wouldn't hurt anything if I took a closer look at the area. Maybe I would see something that the police had missed. Wishful thinking, but I'd give it a shot anyway. The ghosts and cats followed me as I made my way to the area that Charlotte had pointed out. The air felt different now. Though it had been spooky before, now it was even creepier.

The sensation of being watched fell over me. I looked around but saw no one. Why did I feel this way? Was there another ghost? I certainly hoped not. Two plus the haunted cats were all that I could handle at the moment. I especially didn't want to encounter an evil spirit. Charlotte claimed she saw something. A person in the graveyard at this time of the evening? That was unlikely. Only I was crazy enough to come here at this hour. I reached the area on the edge of the graveyard, but the black iron fence stopped me from going any farther.

"The person would have had to climb the fence if they left this way," I said.

"Maybe they did," Charlotte said. "Or maybe the

person is still in the cemetery. I know I saw some-one."

The thought sent a chill down my spine. She seemed convinced that she'd seen someone.

"Even if you did, they're not here now." I turned to go back to the spot where Tyler's body had been found.

A rustling noise caught my attention. I spun around to see who or what was there. Nothing was there. Yes, I was on edge and every little noise made my anxiety spike. I was letting the spooky surroundings get the better of me. I had to calm down. Or better yet, get out of here.

"What was that?" I asked.

"I didn't see a thing, but I sure heard it," Charlotte said.

"I heard it too," Minnie added.

Grandma Pearl meowed.

"Okay, let's go back," I said.

We'd almost reached the area again when another noise caught my attention. I definitely heard something that time.

"Do you know what it sounded like to me?" Charlotte asked.

"No, what?" I asked.

"It sounded like that old iron door on the mausoleum." Charlotte gestured with a tilt of her head.

"Maybe it was the wind," Minnie said.

"Nevertheless, I think you should check it out," Charlotte said.

I suppose it was worth a look, although I assumed
it was just the wind too. When I reached the mausoleum, I realized that the door was open. I thought
I'd pulled it shut when I walked away. I stopped in
my tracks.

"That door wasn't open before," Charlotte whispered.

"No, it wasn't open." Now my anxiety spiked.

Chapter 21

Cookie's Savvy Tips for Vintage Clothing Shopping

═══════════

*Add cute pieces like swimsuits
to your vintage collection.
Retro sunglasses are also a great way
to wear vintage every day.*

Now it was up to me to close the door again. I inched closer to the open door. My heart beat faster and it was even more difficult to breathe. Don't have a panic attack, I reminded myself. It was probably too late for that. The ghosts and cats crept along beside me. Did we think we'd sneak up on whatever was in that mausoleum? I hoped nothing was in there. Maybe Minnie was right and it was just the wind that had blown the door open. Nevertheless, I was about to find out. When I reached the door, I paused. Just as before it was dark inside. Even darker than before. I couldn't see a thing. I pulled out my phone and turned on the light. That cast an ominous glow around the space.

"What did you say?" I looked at Charlotte.

Her eyes widened. "I didn't say a thing. Maybe

you imagined it. Oh great, now you're having hallucinations."

"I thought I heard a whisper," Minnie said.

"See, it wasn't just me who heard it." I moved the light around the space.

"Maybe someone is calling for you," Charlotte said.

"Stop trying to scare me, Charlotte," I said.

"Yes, don't scare us. I'm already terrified enough," Minnie said.

I leaned in closer and shone the light farther inside the room. Cobwebs, old leaves, and probably creatures I didn't even want to know existed adorned the space like Halloween decorations.

"Cookie, I thought you said you weren't going inside there," Charlotte said.

"I'm not. Just looking for the source of the noise, that's all," I said.

"She's too inquisitive for her own good," Minnie said.

The next thing I knew I fell forward, landing on the concrete floor. I'd been pushed so hard that I tumbled all the way inside the dank and dark space. The door slammed shut.

"Cookie, are you all right?" Charlotte asked in a panic.

"Oh, Cookie, how could I let you get hurt like that? Are you okay? I knew I shouldn't let you get too close." Minnie's voice was at an all-time high pitch.

Feeling around on the damp concrete, I managed to retrieve my phone that had been knocked out of my hand during the fall. I scrambled to my feet. At least I hadn't lost my phone. I clutched it even tighter in my hand now. The meowing from the cats echoed from the other side of the door. Minnie and Charlotte were with me in the dark and spooky space. One thing was for sure. There was no way that I fell forward on my own. I'd felt someone's hand on my back. Someone had shoved me into this place. Panic surged through me now. Feeling my way over to the door, I pushed on it, but it didn't budge.

"I can't breathe," I said.

"Don't panic," Charlotte said.

"That's easy for you to say. You can get out of here." I shoved on the door again. "Someone pushed me inside here. Did you see who it was?"

"No, I was watching you," Charlotte said in a raised voice.

"What about you, Minnie?" I asked.

"I watched you too," Minnie said.

"How will I get out of here?"

Charlotte gestured toward my phone. "How about you call for help?"

"Oh yeah." I touched the phone's screen. "There's no service. Why in this day and age do we not have service? It's not 1996."

"Well, you are in a concrete box," Charlotte said.

"Thanks for reminding me," I said. "The space is

definitely getting smaller. I can feel it closing in on me."

"Calm down, Cookie. You're going to hyperventilate," Charlotte said.

"Can you blame me?" I asked. "You're right. I have to stay calm. Panicking will get me nowhere."

I attempted to inhale a deep breath, but it was difficult to catch my breath. It felt as if there wasn't enough air.

"Just take a few deep breaths and you'll feel better," Minnie said.

"That's what I'm trying to do." Finally, I was able to inhale and exhale a few times.

"There. Now don't you feel better?" Charlotte asked.

"Not at all," I said.

"Cookie is terrible under high-stress situations," Charlotte said.

She acted as if this was no big deal. I was essentially buried alive. No one would ever find me here.

I pounded against the door with my fists. The action made no sound. Only my yelling echoed through the chamber. I had no idea if anyone outside could hear me. Now my hands hurt from pounding and it did nothing to free me from this vault. It looked as if my fate was sealed.

"Let me out of here," I screamed again.

"Maybe your grandmother will go for help. She can get Dylan," Minnie said.

I looked at Minnie. "Oh, that's a good point." I released a deep breath. "That makes me feel better."

"Oh sure, what she says helps. What I say you ignore," Charlotte said, tossing her hands up.

A scuffling sound came from somewhere behind me. I screamed and pushed my back against the door. Charlotte and Minnie screeched and stood beside me against the wall. I shone the light in the area where I thought I'd heard the noise. At first I saw nothing, but next it moved. I screamed again, which caused the ghosts to scream. A hissing came from the area and I knew I was in big trouble.

"What is it now? I didn't hear anything," Charlotte said, clutching her chest.

I pointed across the space. "There's a snake."

"Let me out of here," Charlotte screamed.

So much for Charlotte remaining calm. She was currently flipping out. She tried to pound against the door, but her hands went right through the stone. Minnie remained quiet. At least she was keeping it together.

"Charlotte, you do realize that you can go outside any time you want? I'm the one who's trapped in here. Not to mention you're a ghost and the snake can't kill you."

"Oh . . . I forgot. This is your fault, Cookie, for causing such panic," Charlotte said.

"My fault? You got me into this, Charlotte Meadows, and you'd better find a way to get me out of it." I pumped my fist at her.

Charlotte's eyes widened. "Well, I've never."

"You'd better start," I said.

"Ladies, please don't argue." Minnie held her hands up, signaling for us to stop.

I released a deep breath. "Sorry, Charlotte, I guess I'm just panicking too."

"Well, I'm sorry too, Cookie," she said.

"Now that you all made up, what about that?" Minnie pointed at the snake.

"What if the snake is poisonous?" I asked.

"At least you'd know what being a ghost is like," Charlotte said.

"You're not helping."

"Just preparing you, that's all," she said.

"What if the person who pushed me in here also left the snake?" I kept my light pointed at the creature.

So far it hadn't moved, but I was certain it was planning its attack. Would someone have plotted to get me in here and trap me with the snake? Had the person followed me to the graveyard? That was a terrifying thought that sent a shiver down my spine.

"It's a distinct possibility that someone did this on purpose," Charlotte said.

I couldn't wait around and hope that someone saved me. I had to attempt to escape this tomb. If I took the light off the snake would it make its move? That was the chance I'd have to take. Facing the door again, I pounded against it. It wasn't budging, as if someone was holding the other side.

"You're going to break every bone in your hands if you keep doing that," Charlotte said.

"Charlotte, will you go out there and see if some-one is against the door? Maybe they locked it?"

"Gladly," Charlotte said before disappearing out of the space.

I wasn't sure why Charlotte had stayed inside with me for as long as she had. That was what friends did for each other. We might bicker a lot, but I could always count on Charlotte. Thank goodness Minnie stayed with me now. I didn't want to be alone. A couple seconds went by, but it felt like an eternity.

"What is Charlotte doing out there?" I asked.

"Charlotte is right beside you," Charlotte said in my ear. "No one is out there."

I screamed and clutched my chest. Minnie and Charlotte echoed my shriek.

"Will you please not do that?" Charlotte fanned herself. "I can't handle it."

"You're the one who popped up in my ear. Are you trying to give me a heart attack? I thought you were outside. What did you see?"

"I came back in to tell you," Charlotte said. "No one was out there."

"The person must have run away when they pushed you," Minnie said.

I shone the light toward the back on the snake again. It wasn't there. "Oh no, the snake is gone. Where is it?"

Charlotte looked over her shoulder. "Please don't let it attack."

"This is scary. I've definitely let you down," Minnie said.

"Minnie, what are you blathering on about? This is no time for chitchat," Charlotte said.

I moved the light across the dark space. Light pooled along the stone floor. My worst fear had come true. The snake had moved closer to me.

"That thing is poisonous." Charlotte's words had never sounded so terrifying.

That was the last thing I wanted to hear. It wasn't as if I could move farther away. My back was already pressed against the door. There was nowhere to go.

"What did you see out there, Charlotte? Are you sure no one was holding the door? I have to get out of here."

"There's no one against the door. I don't see why it's stuck," Charlotte said with her eyes still focused on the snake.

"I have to get out of here." Panic overtook my body and my arms shook.

The light from my phone wobbled up and down like a light show as my arms moved.

"Cookie, calm down before you pass out in here," Charlotte yelled.

There was no way I was giving up this easily. I had to use all my strength and give this one last shot. Turning around toward the door, I peeked over at the snake. It had slithered even closer to me. This was it. The thing was going to bite me soon. I had to get out of there before it was too late. As much as I could without getting into the snake's path, I moved back a few steps.

"What are you doing, Cookie?" Charlotte asked.

"I'm going to get this door open," I said.

"This doesn't look like a good idea." Minnie's eyes were wide with fear.

"Maybe not, but it is my only chance."

On the count of three I was going to run with all my strength and slam into that door.

"Cookie, you realize that door is solid? You'll break every bone in that little body of yours," Charlotte said.

"It's not as solid as the walls. I just think the latch is stuck. A little bump will work it loose. It's not like I'll knock the door down." My heart thumped harder.

"Okay, as long as you realize you're not Wonder Woman."

One, two, three.

I ran and shoved my body against the door. It broke free, and I tumbled from the tomb and landed on the grass facedown. I groaned. The fresh night air and smell of grass greeted me. I wanted to cry.

"Cookie, are you okay?" Charlotte asked.

"She doesn't look okay," Minnie said.

The ghosts peered down at me. My shoulder hurt, but other than that I thought I was okay. I rolled over onto my back.

"I'm okay." I scanned the area and realized we were alone in the graveyard. "Where are the cats?"

Panic surged through me when I realized Grandma Pearl and Tyler were missing. Since the day Wind Song had shown up at my shop I'd known where she was at all times. Now that I was without her I was panicking. Tyler was grumpy, but I didn't want anything to happen to him.

"Do you see the cats?" I asked as I climbed to my feet.

I brushed off the dirt from my clothing and hands. Grass stains covered the front of my skirt. Now I regretted wearing this, but I was confident I could get the stain out.

"I don't see them anywhere," Charlotte said, looking around the graveyard.

"Here, kitty, kitty," Minnie called out. "Grandma Pearl and Tyler, where are you?"

The slithering noise caught my attention. After spinning around, I backed up a few steps. The snake came out from the mausoleum. With my attention focused on finding the cats I'd almost forgotten about the snake. It moved to the right and slithered away.

I released a deep breath. "Thank goodness that thing is gone. Let's look around and find the cats."

"Maybe they're at the front gate trying to attract someone's attention," Minnie said.

"Now I'd love to see that. What are they waving . . . their paws to flag down a car?" Charlotte chortled.

"It could happen. I bet that's what they're doing," I said.

It was almost completely dark now. At least I could still make my way around the graves with the aid of my phone's light. The wind picked up and leaves scuttled across the ground in front of me. Every slight movement had me on guard. I rushed toward the front. My legs could not move fast enough. When we reached the front gate Dylan's car pulled up.

"What is he doing here?" Charlotte asked.

"I don't know. How did he know I was here?" I asked.

Looking around for the cats, I called out, "Grandma Pearl? Tyler? Wind Song?"

I stood outside the front gate now. I still hadn't spotted the cats, and a sinking feeling had settled in my stomach. Dylan opened his car door and got out. He stood there with the door open.

"What is he doing?" Charlotte asked.

Grandma Pearl and Tyler jumped out of the car. They had left to find Dylan.

"I can't believe it," I said.

Grandma Pearl and Tyler were my heroes. The cats ran over to me. Even Tyler, which surprised me. I picked up Grandma Pearl and hugged her. When I placed her down, I lifted Tyler up into my arms and hugged him too. He moved away and squirmed.

"Okay, you don't like affection, I get it."

He jumped from my arms.

Dylan hurried over to me. "Cookie, what are you doing?"

I blew the hair from my eyes. "I was locked in the mausoleum."

He stared in stunned silence.

"You've finally shocked him silent," Charlotte said.

Dylan shook his head. "How in the world did that happen? Or do I even want to know?"

"I'd go with the 'you don't want to know' option," Charlotte said.

"Someone pushed me inside. Somehow the door was stuck and there was a poisonous snake in there."

"A poisonous snake?" Disbelief filled his words.

"You heard her correctly," Charlotte said.

I shook my head. "Yes, a poisonous snake."

"How did you get out?" he asked.

"I rammed my body into the door and the latch came unstuck. I can't believe the cats came to find you. But how did you know where I was? They can't talk to you," I said.

Little did he know the cats really could talk.

"They talked to me the same way that they talk to you." Dylan studied my face.

"What did he just say?" Charlotte asked.

There was no way that he knew about the cats.

"What do you mean?" I asked.

"The cats use the board to talk with you," Dylan said, staring directly at me.

"I don't understand," I said.

"Don't play innocent, Cookie. He means he used the Ouija board," Charlotte said.

My eyes widened. "You used the Ouija board?"

Dylan smiled. "I had to do it. They came to give me a message, so I knew it was important."

"This guy is pretty cool." Charlotte pointed at Dylan.

"Grandma Pearl spelled out the word *graveyard*, so I knew that must be where you were," Dylan said.

"I would have liked to have seen that," Charlotte said.

"This is incredible," Minnie said.

"I bet you were surprised when you saw the cats," I said.

"The cats were just walking down the street. I recognized them right away and knew something was wrong," Dylan said.

"Where did you find a Ouija board?" I asked.

Dylan shrugged. "I made one. Just used some paper."

"Whatever works. He improvises. I like that," Charlotte said.

"Now that you have found the cats you need to figure out who pushed you," Minnie said.

Dylan wrapped his arm around my shoulders. "Let's get you out of here."

"What about the person who pushed me?" I asked.

Dylan looked me in the eyes. "Are you sure someone pushed you?"

I studied his face. "Well, I'm not positive, but I can't see how I would have fallen forward."

He pushed hair off my cheek. "You have been known to be a bit clumsy."

Charlotte scoffed. "A bit? She has two left feet."

"I don't think that was the case this time," Minnie said.

"Did you see anyone?" Dylan asked.

I shook my head. "No, I never saw anyone."

"I did see someone," Charlotte said.

"That's right. Charlotte saw someone," I said.

"Who did she see?" Dylan asked.

"If I knew that we might know who pushed Cookie," Charlotte said.

"Well, it was just out of the corner of her eye, so she's not sure," I said.

"I know by the look on his face that he doesn't believe me," Charlotte said. "Tell him I'm not happy with him."

I sighed. "Charlotte isn't happy with you."

Dylan quirked an eyebrow and looked around. "Why isn't she happy with me? What did I do?"

I pointed. "She's right there. Charlotte isn't happy because you don't believe her."

He turned his attention to Charlotte. "Sorry, Ms. Meadows, I believe that you saw something, but it could have been a bird, or a cat."

"Or a ghost!" Minnie said.

Charlotte placed her hands on her hips. "It was a person."

"You just need some rest." Dylan took me by the arm.

"And furthermore, it's Charlotte. Don't call me Ms. Meadows," Charlotte said behind Dylan's back. "He acts like he doesn't know me at all."

Dylan guided me over to my car with my gang of friends trailing behind us. The cats, ghosts, and I got into my car. This time I was in the passenger seat and Charlotte was forced to sit in the back. She didn't complain this time. Dylan knew I wouldn't want to leave my car behind.

"I'll have someone drive me back for my car," he said, starting the Buick's engine.

"True love is when Cookie allows someone to drive her car," Charlotte said.

"It is sweet of him," Minnie said.

As Dylan drove away from the curb I peered out the window at the graveyard. It looked peaceful and hauntingly beautiful under the glow of the moon. It had been anything but peaceful while I'd been there. Was someone stalking and harassing me? I felt as if the snake had been in there on purpose. I was tired though and maybe my mind was overwhelmed with racing thoughts because of my exhaustion.

Dylan was right. I needed rest. Though I couldn't help but wonder if the killer was after me. On the other hand, I had been in a graveyard. It could have been a deadly threat from the spirit world. If I wasn't careful, a photo shoot might not be the only shots fired. I had to solve the case before it was too late.

Chapter 22

Charlotte's Tips for a Fabulous Afterlife
=======

The living won't always ask for help.
Sometimes you just have to give it without solicitation.

The next morning over breakfast, I jotted down notes of what I knew about the case. Tina Fairchild was Tyler's ex-girlfriend and definitely on the suspect list. According to Tyler's friends, Tina had been stalking Tyler and the other models. Apparently, she hadn't accepted their breakup and wanted Tyler back.

"What are you doing?" Charlotte asked from over my shoulder.

"Taking notes on the murder case, what else?" I tapped my pen against the pad of paper.

"A little light work over breakfast, huh? Nothing like thinking about bloody violence while enjoying a bowl of Cheerios." Charlotte sat down beside me.

"All of the models," I said as I continued to write. "And the model's boyfriend Darrin."

"Don't forget the mystery woman Shanna Sizemore," Charlotte said.

Minnie shuffled into the kitchen as if she'd just

woken up. As far as I knew the ghosts didn't sleep. Charlotte usually spent that time on the other side with her boyfriend. Was that where Minnie had been too?

I finished my bite of cereal and said, "How could I forget Shanna?"

"If you don't stop making your list you'll be late for work," Charlotte said.

"You're right. I let time slip away." I jumped up from the table and put my bowl in the sink.

Now I had to hurry and dress so I wouldn't have to speed to town. The last thing I needed was a ticket from Dylan. Today I felt like dressing up more than usual. Maybe because I thought it would lift my spirits. No pun intended.

I pulled out a special Chanel dress that I'd never worn. It was sleeveless with a pink form-fitted skirt and a white tank style on the upper part of the dress. My mother had discovered this when we were estate sale shopping near my parents' house. I'd been saving it for a special occasion. If I waited around for that, though, I might never get a chance to wear it. Today was as good a day as any. I figured I should seize the day.

"You're going to wear that?" Charlotte asked from over my shoulder.

She routinely stood behind me at the closet and critiqued my daily outfit selection.

"What's wrong with this dress? It's gorgeous," I said as I held it up to examine.

"You never want to wear it because you're afraid that you'll stain it or ruin it."

"It's a beautiful dress," Minnie said.

"Well, today I feel differently. Things are made to be used and enjoyed." I admired the dress again.

"She must be sick," Charlotte whispered to Minnie.

"Like I said, it is a beautiful dress, Cookie. I think you should wear it," Minnie said.

"Oh go ahead, but don't cry to me when it's ruined." Charlotte studied her fingernails.

"I promise not to cry to you, Charlotte," I said.

After dressing I slipped into my black Chanel flats and grabbed the black quilted Chanel mini flap bag I'd scored off the internet for a great price. I headed for the door.

"Don't you think that's a bit much Chanel?" Charlotte asked.

Normally I would have said yes, but with this outfit I thought it worked. It wasn't as if the labels were plastered everywhere on my outfit.

"Nope," I said as I marched for the door.

"She's in a sassy mood today. Look out," Charlotte said with a click of her tongue.

The cats and ghosts followed me to the car. I peered over at the police car. With his eyes closed and head leaned back against the seat, it looked as if the officer was sleeping. Again. He'd slept yesterday too.

"Should I wake him?" I asked.

"That would be embarrassing for him," Charlotte said. "I'm sure things will be fine. You're just going into town to the shop. He'll wake up and see the car is gone and come find you."

"I'm not sure this is a good idea," Minnie said. "After all, someone did try to get Cookie at her shop."

Charlotte waved her hand. "It'll be fine."

So I slipped behind the wheel and cranked the engine. The officer slept through that so I pulled away from the curb. With the sun shining down on me I cruised the roads toward town. The Flamingos played on the radio.

"This is a beautiful day," I said. "I have a feeling that nothing can go wrong."

Charlotte grimaced. I took the hint that she didn't share my sentiment. She was the one who said everything would be fine.

"If you say so, but never let yourself get too confident," she said.

The blue sky stretched out endlessly. Traffic was light as there were no other cars in front of me. When I glanced in the rearview mirror though there was a black car with darkly tinted windows directly behind me. The windows were so dark that I couldn't see who was behind the wheel.

The next thing I knew, the car bumped me. I wasn't expecting it, so the jolt sent my car to the right. I tried to control the wheel and keep from hitting the ditch, but it was impossible. My car smashed into the ditch. For a short time the world spun. I suppose it was the shock from what had happened. The car sped past and didn't seem concerned with what they'd done. I looked beside me to see if the cats were okay. They stared at me in stunned silence. Thank goodness they were all right.

"Are you all right, Cookie?" Charlotte asked with panic in her voice.

"I'm okay, but my car isn't." I looked around with shock.

"Your car can be fixed, but you can't," Minnie said from the backseat.

"Truer words have never been spoken," Charlotte said.

Trying to get out of the car, I had to shove the door to get it open. Even though the car was slanted in the ditch, I managed to free myself. After climbing out, I moved around to the front of the car. The cats jumped out too. Charlotte and Minnie were already waiting at the front of the car. By the looks on their faces I assumed it wasn't good news.

Standing in front of the car, I stared at the fender, hood, and headlights. It was definitely smashed. Viewing the dents and scratches was actually a painful sight. Luckily, it could be repaired. The damage could have been much worse.

"I know you're upset about the car, but like Minnie said, it can be fixed. The most important thing to worry about is why that person hit your car. They wanted to harm you," Charlotte said.

Now was when the real panic set in. "You're right, Charlotte. That was no accident."

I hurried back to the car for my phone. Charlotte

and Minnie rushed along beside me. The cats were in front of me. They jumped up onto the seat while I reached for my phone. I had to call Dylan.

When he answered the first thing I said was, "I'm okay."

"What happened?" Dylan asked.

"I had an accident, but like I said, I'm fine. The car, not so much." I looked down the road to see if any other cars were coming.

I was all alone out here. For now I considered that a good thing. I didn't want the car that had run me off the road to return.

"Where are you?" he asked. "Where is the officer who was supposed to be with you?"

"Highway 205. I was heading to work. He was asleep in the car so I left him."

Dylan groaned.

"I'm near that old barn. The one that's falling down," I said.

"I'll be there soon," Dylan said.

"Thank goodness he's coming to help," Charlotte said.

"It's a good thing Dylan can help. What would you do without him?" Minnie asked.

"First of all she would call a wrecker," Charlotte said.

Mostly I tried to tune out the ghosts' chatter. Right now I was trying to wrap my head around what had happened. One minute I was cruising along, and the next I was standing out here in the middle of farmland. An uneasy feeling remained with me. I knew I wouldn't be able to shake it off for some time. Moving back to the front of the car, I stared at the dent in the front passenger side of the car.

Thank goodness a couple minutes later Dylan sped down the road. He rolled up to a stop along the road behind my car. The blue lights on his car swirled, but he shut off the siren before he got out.

Dylan jumped out of his car and ran over to me. "Are you hurt?"

I waved my hand. "It was just a fender bender really."

"More like a fender crusher," Charlotte said.

"Why didn't you wake Officer Morrison?" Dylan asked.

"I didn't think there was a reason for him to follow me." I stared at Dylan's face.

"Or so you thought." Charlotte scoffed.

"Cookie was terribly wrong on that one," Minnie said.

"You thought that was a good idea?" Dylan's brow furrowed.

"At the time it seemed like it." I was ready for Dylan to yell at me.

Instead he gave me a disappointed look, which was much worse than being yelled at. I'd rather have him yelling at me.

"You've really done it this time, Cookie," Charlotte said, shaking her head.

Dylan stepped to the front of the car. "Did an

animal run out in front of the car? Is that why you swerved?" He grimaced as he inspected the damage.

Charlotte scoffed. "I wish that was all that had happened. You have to tell him how it happened now. Tell him everything, Cookie."

"Don't leave out a single detail," Minnie said.

The cats meowed in agreement.

When I didn't answer right away, Dylan turned to me. "What happened, Cookie?"

"Cookie, you have to tell him everything. Right now," Charlotte demanded.

"Yes, you simply must," Minnie said.

After another few seconds, I said, "Someone hit my car and made me run off into the ditch."

Just speaking the words made me shiver with fear all over again. Saying it out loud made it all the more real that someone had done this on purpose.

Dylan ran his hand through his hair. "Oh, Cookie, I was worried something like this would happen. That killer is still on the loose and obviously becoming more unhinged by the day."

"That's why I'm trying to find out who did this," I said. "I managed to get the last part of the license plate on the car."

"Telling the police not to follow you isn't the way to find out who did this," Dylan said.

"It's a way to get yourself killed," Charlotte said.

I glared at her.

"I just didn't want to be a pain. Plus, I don't like having a babysitter."

"You didn't want anyone to tell me what you were doing," Dylan said.

"That too," I said.

Dylan stared at me. "You got the license plate number?"

"Only the last part," I said.

"That's a start. I'll call to have the car towed." Dylan pulled out his phone.

"Cookie, you have to listen to what Dylan says," Charlotte said.

Minnie nodded. "Yes, you really should."

I narrowed my eyes. "This was your idea, Charlotte. And you encouraged it, Minnie."

She looked down at her cream-colored shoes but didn't answer.

Dylan ended the call. "It's taken care of."

"Thank you, Dylan. I really appreciate everything you do for me."

He hugged me. "Just don't worry me, okay?"

"Can I get a ride to work?" I asked with a smile.

Dylan took me by the hand. "You scared me. I raced here so fast I'm surprised I didn't get a speeding ticket."

"It's a good thing he had those lights and siren," Charlotte said.

After saying good-bye to the Buick as the wrecker towed it to the local repair shop, I was grateful I had Dylan to drive me to work.

"I don't like being in the backseat of a police car," Charlotte said through the partition.

"Now I remember," Minnie yelled.

I jumped at her loud statement.

"For heaven's sake, you scared the bejesus out of me." Charlotte stared at Minnie.

"Now I remember . . . I wasn't murdered. It was an accident. I drove right off the road during a rainstorm."

"That's awful, Minnie," I said.

"At least I know I wasn't murdered," she said.

"And I thought we had so much in common," Charlotte said.

"I remember I was driving to work at Adler's Department Store . . . cars were still a relatively new thing."

"A working girl . . . okay, so we have that in common. Just like Cookie too." Charlotte winked.

"I was single too," Minnie said.

"Cookie won't be that way for long." Charlotte wiggled her eyebrows.

During the rest of the drive I explained to Dylan what Minnie had said about her accident. I suppose what had happened to me had sparked her memory.

Dylan walked me to the door. "How about lunch today?"

"Sounds great. Call me when you're ready. Thank you again for everything."

Dylan leaned down and kissed me. "I love you, Cookie Chanel."

My body tingled and the smile on my face was instant. "I love you too, Dylan Valentine."

He walked backward a few steps and watched me.

"He's going to run into a lamppost," Minnie said.

"He has that goofy lovestruck look on his face," Charlotte said.

Dylan turned around and headed toward his car. I watched him for a few more seconds until I spotted movement out of the corner of my eye. Heather was standing at the front door of her shop. She smiled and waved.

As Dylan drove away she walked over. "You two lovebirds look happy today."

"After what happened you wouldn't think I'd be so happy, right?" I watched Dylan pull away from the curb.

She frowned. "What happened?"

"Oh yeah, I haven't told you yet. I wrecked my car," I said nonchalantly.

"What?" Heather's voice went up an octave.

Charlotte plugged her ears with her index fingers. "Why are you so loud?"

Heather waved off Charlotte's comment. "Tell me what happened. Were you injured?"

Heather touched my arms and head, looking for blood.

"No injuries. A car bumped me and ran me off the road," I said with a wave of my hand.

Heather's eyes widened. "Cookie, this is scary. You're sure you weren't hurt?"

"I wasn't hurt, but I can't say the same for the car," I said around a sigh.

"The car can be fixed. If you're hurt you might not be able to be fixed."

"That's exactly what I told her," Charlotte said.

"Do you know who it was?" Heather asked.

"I have no idea, but Dylan is on the lookout." I shoved the key into the front door lock. "I managed to get the last numbers on the license plate as the car drove by."

"I hope they catch the person soon," Heather said.

"Me too," I said.

Movement caught my attention. Across the street two women stood facing each other talking. Normally this wouldn't have been out of the ordinary. This time though I was more than a little intrigued. One of the women was Shanna. I didn't recognize who she was speaking with.

Charlotte noticed her at the same time. "That's Shanna. The woman who Tyler had a date with when he was murdered."

Heather nodded. "I remember."

"What is she doing?" Minnie asked, her voice barely above a whisper.

We stood in silence, watching the women talk. After a few more seconds they stopped talking, and the unknown woman crossed the street. She was headed this way. Shanna walked in the opposite direction. I had to know what they'd been talking about. Though I suppose they were just friends and this was a friendly conversation. They'd probably spotted each other on the sidewalk and stopped to say hello. Nevertheless, as the woman walked down the sidewalk toward us, I decided to stop her.

"She's headed this way. I'm going to ask her," I said.

Another woman was walking down the street toward us. "Here comes my appointment. You'll let me know what happens?" Heather asked.

"As soon as I find out," I said.

Heather hurried toward her shop.

When the woman who'd been talking with Shanna drew near, I said, "Excuse me. I hate to bother you, but that woman you were speaking with. Her name is Shanna, right?"

I smiled, hoping she would realize I wasn't crazy. The dark-haired woman peered over her shoulder as if she was searching for Shanna.

When she turned to me again she frowned. "Shanna? No, her name is Tina Fairchild."

I wouldn't have been more shocked if this woman had punched me in the stomach. It was as if the wind had been knocked out of me. Charlotte and Minnie gasped. I recognized the name *Tina Fairchild* and so did they. Tina had been the woman I'd been looking for. She was Tyler's ex-girlfriend.

"Her name isn't Shanna?" I asked.

The woman shook her head. "No, is everything okay?"

I chuckled. "I guess she looks like Shanna."

"Way to play it off, Cookie," Charlotte said.

The woman smiled. "It's easy to mistake people sometimes."

"This is a big mistake," Charlotte said. "Only I have

a feeling it wasn't a mistake on Shanna's part. Or whatever her name is."

"I agree," Minnie said.

That made three of us.

"Are you friends with Tina?" I asked.

Now the woman really would think I was strange for asking. Nevertheless, I needed all the information I could get.

"We know each other from college. I was shocked to see her in Sugar Creek," the woman said.

"Shocked to see her?" Charlotte said. "With Tyler here I think we know why Tina was in Sugar Creek."

"Did she say why she was here?" I asked.

"Just that she was visiting a friend. She didn't say who the friend was."

"Oh, we know who that friend was," Charlotte said.

"Actually, Tina seemed vague about it. Is Tina in some kind of trouble?" the woman asked with a frown.

"She must know your boyfriend is a detective," Charlotte said.

"I think she knows someone I know," I said.

"Shanna?" the woman asked.

Charlotte laughed.

"Yes, Shanna," I said.

"Well, Tina said she was going into that shop on the corner. Maybe you can catch her." The woman pointed.

"Thank you," I said.

"Best of luck," the woman said as she turned and walked away.

"Well, what are you waiting for? You'd better get over there and ask Tina what this is all about," Charlotte said.

"Sorry, Grandma Pearl and Tyler, you'll have to stay at the shop while I check this out. Other stores probably won't allow you in." I opened my shop door and the cats paused. "I'll come back as soon as I can."

Thank goodness they decided against being stubborn and walked inside. I shut and locked the door behind them.

"Okay, let's go." I motioned for the ghosts to follow me.

Sometimes I forget the ghosts were around. I'd grown so used to speaking with Charlotte that it was like having a living person with me. Luckily, I didn't notice anyone watching me this time, but I'd have to be more careful. The ghosts followed me as I rushed across the street. My pace was brisk as I hurried toward the shop on the corner. However, before I reached the door, I spotted Tina walking out.

"There she is," Charlotte said with excitement.

"I want to get her attention, but I don't know what to call her," I said. "I'm guessing *hey you* won't work."

"Call her by her real name, Tina. You need to let her know that you know the truth," Charlotte said.

"That could be dangerous. What if she's the killer?" I asked.

"Please be careful, Cookie, and don't get hurt,

because I don't know what I'm doing," Minnie said in a shaky voice.

"There you go again, Minnie, talking weird. This is about Cookie right now." Charlotte waved her hand.

"It's just that I'm supposed to . . ." Minnie's words were cut off when Charlotte held up her hand.

"This is about Cookie. Anyway, Tina can't do anything to you right here on the street . . . can she?" Charlotte asked.

"Anything is possible," I said.

"Okay, use Shanna," Charlotte said. "For heaven's sake, use a name. 'Hey you' will work at this point. Don't let her get away."

"Shanna," I called out.

Tina didn't turn around.

"I guess she forgot she was using that name," Charlotte said. "She's getting into that car. You'll never catch her now."

"Maybe she is ignoring Cookie," Minnie said.

"She's getting away and I don't have a car," I said in a panic. "Wait. I can borrow Heather's car."

"I don't think you have time for that," Charlotte said.

"I have to give it a shot," I said, running across the street toward Heather's shop.

After opening the door, I burst through. Heather was sitting at the table toward the back of the room with a client. They stopped the tarot card reading and stared at me. Heather's client looked as if she was terrified. Like she thought I was there to rob the store.

"Sorry for interrupting," I said, trying to catch my breath.

Heather knew that something was wrong. I'd never run into her shop like that.

"Is everything okay?" Heather asked.

The woman sitting across from Heather stared at me too.

"Can I borrow your car?" I asked.

"Of course." Heather pushed to her feet. "Excuse me. I'll be right back."

The woman gave a half-hearted smile. "Take your time."

I rushed to the front of the store while Heather got her keys. I peered out the door window to see if Tina was still in sight. Of course she was gone by now. Would I really be able to catch up with her? Probably not.

When Heather handed the keys to me, I said, "No time to explain right now. I promise I won't wreck your car."

Heather called out as I dashed out the door. "Be careful."

The odds of catching up to Tina now were slim, but I had to take the chance.

Chapter 23

Cookie's Savvy Tips for Vintage Clothing Shopping

*With so many great vintage dresses,
it would be a shame to overlook them
when shopping for party wear.*

I jumped into Heather's Prius. Compared to the size of my car this was like sitting in a toy car. The ghosts seemed so much closer to me now. I liked having the extra space that my car provided.

Charlotte shifted in the front seat, as if that would somehow magically make it bigger. "This car is just like your mother's. Heather's more like your mother than you."

I buckled my seat belt and pushed the gas.

"Are you sure this thing works?" Charlotte asked with a frown.

"It just doesn't have the get-up-and-go that my Buick has," I said, looking at the speedometer.

"We would get there faster if you'd borrowed one of the lawn mowers from the Tractor Supply store," Charlotte said.

Minnie laughed from the confined backseat as if that was one of the funniest things she'd ever heard. Charlotte and I glanced back at her. She was still laughing.

"What's gotten into her?" Charlotte asked.

"I think the stress has caused her to crack," I said as I headed down Main Street.

I hoped Tina hadn't turned on a side street. That was a chance I'd have to take. There were a few cars up ahead, but I hadn't spotted the Ford Focus that Tina was driving. My phone alerted me to a text message. I glanced down and saw that it was from Dylan.

> Found the car that ran you off the road. It had been
> stolen from Hagerty's Drugstore parking lot and
> abandoned on Route Four. I'm headed to your
> shop now.

There was no way I could answer him at the moment.

"Don't get a speeding ticket," Charlotte said.

Minnie laughed again. "You wouldn't get one on the lawn mower."

"Do you see her?" I asked.

"I've got my eye out," Charlotte said.

"Me too," Minnie said.

At least she'd stopped laughing.

Charlotte focused her attention on me again.

"What?" I asked as I clutched the steering wheel with both hands.

"You driving a Prius just seems wrong. I can't see you in anything but your Buick," Charlotte said.

"I can see her on the lawn mower." Minnie howled with laughter again.

"Minnie, it wasn't that funny. Knock it off," Charlotte said.

Minnie stopped laughing and focused her attention on Charlotte.

"With any luck I'll have my car back soon," I said.

I'd reached the edge of downtown now. There was still no sign of Tina. My hope was fading fast. I was almost ready to give up on finding her when I spotted the car up ahead stopped at a red light.

"There she is," I said excitedly.

"Good job, Cookie. Now get her." Charlotte pointed.

The light turned green as I approached, and Tina made a left turn. I was a couple cars behind her, but I was able to keep up at a good distance so that she wouldn't see me.

"Did you see the gas gauge?" Charlotte gestured.

"No, why?"

"You have a problem," Charlotte said. "Does this thing have a battery?"

"Oh no," Minnie said.

I looked at the gauge. It was almost at the empty level. Ugh. Heather was always forgetting to put gas in her car. I'd have to chance it though. There was no time to stop and fill up.

"I wonder where Tina's going," Charlotte said.

Wherever she was headed, it was away from town and getting less populated.

"There's not much out this way," I said. "Plus, the interstate is in the other direction."

"The only thing this way is that nature preserve," Charlotte said.

"Why would she go there?" I asked.

"Your guess is as good as mine." Charlotte sat up straight on the seat.

Another car turned off. Now there was only one car between Tina and me. I hoped that she didn't notice the Prius following her. Though she would look for a Buick and not a Prius. The thought hit me. What if she knew my car was wrecked? Maybe she had been responsible for it. No, the car that ran me off the road was black. Dylan said the car had been stolen and then abandoned. Tina might have stolen that car just to use in an attempt to make me wreck.

As I drove along I thought about Tina using a fake name. This certainly explained why I'd never been able to speak with Tina, and why I'd gotten the strange vibe from Shanna. She'd fooled everyone.

"Wait. She's stopping," Charlotte said.

"I hope she doesn't realize you're following her," Minnie said.

I eased off the gas and pulled over to the side of the road.

"Don't let her get away," Charlotte said.

The pressure was mounting. If Tina got away we might never catch her again. Tina turned down another isolated and narrow road. After a few seconds, I merged back onto the road and drove to where she'd turned. Right away I spotted Tina's car pulled over to the side of the road. I turned down the street too. I kept my speed to a minimum since I hadn't spotted Tina yet. What was she doing?

"What will you do now?" Charlotte asked.

"I have to confront her," I said.

"Oh, that's not creepy. You followed this woman all the way to this remote area. She'll think you're a stalker," Charlotte said.

"It does seem that way," Minnie said.

"She'll have to get over it," I said as I pulled the Prius up behind her car.

"She's not even in the car," Charlotte said.

I scanned the area. "Where is she?"

"This is so bizarre," Charlotte said.

"I get a bad feeling about this, Cookie," Minnie said.

I shut off the engine and got out of the car, peering around at the dense trees. Birds chirped in the distance and sun filtered through the branches. It felt as if I was completely shut off from the world. Still there was no sign of Tina. She must have gone into the woods.

"What if there was another car that picked her up?" I asked.

"I think this is a dead-end road," Charlotte said. "The car would have turned around and come back this way."

I walked over to Tina's car for a closer look. Peering inside, I saw nothing unusual. Not only was there nothing out of the ordinary, there was actually nothing in the car. No purse, keys, nothing.

"She's neat," Charlotte said as she stood beside me.

"Look. There's a path over there." Minnie pointed. "Do you think she went that way?"

"I'd say that was the only way she could have gone," I said, moving around the car toward the path.

"There is no way you are walking down that path by yourself," Charlotte said, stepping in front of me.

I had to stop to keep from walking right through her.

"Why not?" I asked with my hands on my hips.

"Because it's like she is luring you into the forest."

"Oh, Charlotte. Sometimes you let your imagination get the better of you," I said.

She raised an eyebrow. "Do I? Tell me that there isn't a possibility she could be doing this on purpose. Go ahead, I'll wait."

I inhaled and released a deep breath. "Of course there is a possibility, but I can take care of myself."

"Tyler thought the same thing." She held her hands up. "I can't let you do this."

"She has a good point," Minnie said.

"I have to go in there, and there's nothing you can do to stop me," I said.

Charlotte stood right in front of me with her hands on her hips, as if that was really going to stop me. She didn't budge. I raised an eyebrow. She looked determined, but she forgot about the little detail of her being a ghost. I stepped forward and walked right through her.

"Ugh. I hate when you do that," she said.

Moving through her had left me with cold chills even though the temperature was still warm outside.

"Sorry, Charlotte, it had to be done." I headed down the path toward the woods.

The only sounds came from the birds high in the trees and the leaves and pine needles that crunched under my feet. It was cooler and darker under the shade of the trees. Charlotte and Minnie followed me down the path. My anxiety increased with each step. I wouldn't let Charlotte know though. She would just remind me that this was a bad idea.

A short distance down the path and a snapping noise caught my attention. I froze on the spot.

"What was that?" I whispered.

"It was probably just a branch falling," Charlotte said. "Don't you dare get scared now. This was your idea."

"It's okay, Cookie, I'll protect you. That's what I'm here for," Minnie said.

Charlotte and I looked at her.

"There you go being weird again, Minnie," Charlotte said.

After a few more seconds with no other sounds, I continued down the path. There was no sign of Tina. The more I walked into the wooded area the more I thought Charlotte might have been right. Fear had me in its clutches now.

I wouldn't go much farther before I turned

around and headed back for the car. Even if Charlotte would be smug about the fact that she was right. Only a couple more steps and someone grabbed me from behind. The shock of it sucked the air from my lungs. I fell to the ground, struggling to break free from the person's tight grip. Leaves and branches cracked and popped underneath the weight of my body and the struggle.

"Cookie, you have to get away from her," Charlotte yelled.

I hadn't seen the face of the person who had attacked me yet. Since Charlotte said "she" I assumed it was Tina. The person was still behind me though, so I couldn't be sure. Was this Tina? It had to be since no one else would be out here in the woods. I managed to turn enough to see her face. It was Tina. A look of ice-cold fury covered her face. Tina reached down and pulled me to my feet.

"What do you think you're doing following me like that?" she asked with venom in her voice.

Before I had a chance to answer she swung a huge branch at me. I ducked and managed to miss the impact from her improvised weapon.

"You have to find something to hit her with," Charlotte said.

"There are branches over here," Minnie yelled.

I didn't want to fight with Tina. Though I had to get away from her. Obviously she was crazy.

"I knew you would follow me," Tina said.

"See, I told you this was a setup," Charlotte said.

"There is no time for 'I told you so,' Charlotte," I said.

Tina cast a strange look my way and asked, "You just don't know when to stop, do you?"

"You've gotten yourself into a real pickle this time," Charlotte said with a shake of her head.

"We have to do something," Minnie said with panic in her voice.

I moved my arms and tried to kick. Out of the corner of my eye I spotted the ghosts. I had no idea what they were doing. It looked as if they were trying to move a branch. Maybe they would distract Tina long enough so that I could get away. Somehow I managed to break free from her hold. She was stronger than I imagined. There wasn't a chance to get away from her though. In a split second she pulled out a gun and aimed it at me.

"Cookie, she has a gun," Charlotte yelled.

"Yes, I see that, Charlotte."

I didn't even pretend that I wasn't talking to the ghosts. I even looked over at Charlotte. What was the point if Tina was going to shoot me anyway?

"Oh dear. This doesn't look good. I've failed at my job," Minnie said.

"Your job?" Charlotte repeated what I was thinking.

"Yes, I'm Cookie's guardian angel. The whole reason I'm here was to help her. This isn't helping her."

"I have a guardian angel?" I asked out loud.

Tina scoffed. "I don't think you do. There is no

angel coming to save you from this situation. You brought this on yourself."

"I really don't like this woman," Charlotte said. "Come on, Minnie, we have to try to move this branch. This is no time to give up."

Charlotte and Minnie went back to trying to move the branch. Bless their hearts, I really appreciated the attempt, but I knew it was hopeless.

"Why are you doing this?" I asked.

"I told you because you wouldn't stop trying to find out who killed Tyler." Tina aimed the gun directly at me.

Though her hand shook. The only hope I had was that she wasn't a good aim.

Chapter 24

Charlotte's Tips for a Fabulous Afterlife

———————

*It gives me great satisfaction
when I've been proven correct.
That's why I give advice without being asked for it.*

"Why did you kill Tyler?" I asked.

Tina's face was now twisted with an evil grin. "Because if I can't have him then no one can."

"Oh, that's a healthy way to look at it," Charlotte said sarcastically.

How was I going to get the gun away from Tina? Could I somehow knock it out of her hand? I'd have to get closer.

"Why did you pretend to be Shanna?" I asked.

"Tyler wasn't talking to me anymore," Tina said.

"That's understandable. I wouldn't want to talk with you anymore either," I said.

"You think this is funny?" Tina asked. "I'll show you just how funny it is."

"Don't make her angry, Cookie," Charlotte said. "What have I done? I've created a monster with my sarcastic ways."

Charlotte was right. I suppose I shouldn't be

sarcastic with the woman who had a gun pointed at me. It was a little too late for that now though.

"You can put this all behind you now, you know? It doesn't have to end this way," I said, trying to sound as if Tina was a friend.

I was pretty sure that Tina wasn't falling for it though. This would end with Tina going to jail if I ever got away from this. Though I didn't see any hope of that happening. I seriously doubted I would be able to talk her out of killing me.

"Yeah, right. You will tell the police that I killed Tyler." Her eyes narrowed as her hand shook even more.

How would I answer that? Yes, I would tell the police. I'd be crazy not to tell them. Plus, she probably knew that Dylan was my boyfriend.

"I'm sure if you explained to the police," I said.

That was a vague answer.

"That never works," Tina said.

Minnie and Charlotte were still focused on the tree branch.

"You can get a lawyer," I said.

"That's not happening," Tina said. "There is only one way out of this."

At least if she killed me out here I knew that Dylan would come looking for me. Wait. I was in the woods. How long would it take for him to find me? Heather's car was parked out there on the road, so that would be helpful. A million terrible thoughts ran through my mind.

To think I came into the woods on purpose. Now all I wanted to do was find my way out of there. Just my luck I'd come face-to-face with Tina. She had the gun and wanted to kill me. She probably figured that killing me was the only way she could keep from going to jail. No doubt when Tyler found out Tina was pretending to be Shanna she felt she had to murder him too.

A cracking sound came from my right. Tina looked over at the branch that Charlotte and Minnie had finally been able to throw. This was my only chance and I had to take it. I lunged forward and tackled Tina, as if we were playing in the Super Bowl. She never knew what hit her. Tina groaned as she hit the ground with a thud. The gun flew from her hand. Another groan escaped her as I jumped up and dashed for the weapon. With a shaky hand I aimed the weapon at her. Her eyes were wide as she stared at me.

"Isn't she surprised?" Charlotte said with a smirk.

I wasn't sure what to do now. My legs and arms shook. Everything was spinning around me, and I wondered if I would soon pass out. I needed to call for help. The phone wouldn't work out here though. Plus, I didn't want to lower the gun to get my phone from my pocket. If I allowed myself to be distracted at all she would take that opportunity to try to get the gun back from me.

"You can't stand there with the gun pointed at her all day," Charlotte said.

"I think she's regaining her strength," Minnie said.

"You're right, Charlotte," I said.

Tina frowned. "Who's Charlotte?"

"You're confusing her. She thinks you've lost your marbles. If a crazy woman thinks you're crazy you really are in trouble," Charlotte said.

"I'm talking to the ghost that's here with me. Actually, there are two ghosts. Well, one says she's my guardian angel."

"That's right," Minnie said with a smile.

"You really are crazy, aren't you?" Tina said.

"Maybe I am crazy, but I didn't murder anyone. Now get up," I said, motioning with the gun.

"Don't wave that thing around like that," Charlotte said. "Though you have to use more authority in your voice, Cookie. Let her know you mean business."

I gestured again. "Move it."

Tina got up from the ground. If looks could kill I would be a goner.

"Okay, now walk." I motioned with the gun even though Charlotte had told me not to.

Tina walked toward the road where we'd left the cars parked. I followed along behind her with the gun still aimed at her. I had no idea if I could pull the trigger or not. I hoped it didn't come down to that. While she wasn't looking, I pulled the phone from my pocket. It still wasn't working.

"I doubt you would actually shoot me," Tina said with smugness in her voice.

"My father taught me how to fire a gun. I have no problem using it," I said.

"Is that true, Cookie?" Minnie asked.

I shook my head no. Tina didn't have to know the truth.

"That's okay. I'm sure you can use it if you have to," Minnie said.

"Cookie is tough. She'll figure it out," Charlotte said.

When we reached the road, Tina looked around.

"Don't even think about trying to run away," I said.

"I wouldn't dream of it." Her eyes were icy cold as she stared at me.

Within seconds the sirens sounded in the distance. Thank goodness this would all be over soon.

"Oh, we're saved," Charlotte said. "I thought for sure you were finished."

"I thought you had confidence in me?" I asked.

"No, I just said that so you wouldn't freak out," Charlotte said with a wave of her hand.

"You are crazy," Tina said.

"Yeah, well, crazy attracts crazy," I said.

Charlotte laughed. "Good one, Cookie."

Minnie howled with laughter again. "Yes, good one, Cookie."

I suppose thinking that the police were headed this way made me let my guard down. The gun was relaxed though, still aimed at Tina. I took my eyes off her for a second and she sprinted toward her car.

"Oh, Cookie, she's getting away," Charlotte called out.

We all took off running.

"Shoot her," Charlotte yelled.

"I can't shoot her for running," I said between breaths.

I pumped my legs as fast as I could, which sadly wasn't that fast. Tina opened her car door just as I reached her. I stretched my arm forward and made contact with her shirt.

She yelled. "Get off me."

Tina swung her arm and tried to hit me, but she missed. Yes, I still had the gun. At this point I was afraid Tina might actually try to get it away from me and use it on me. With all my strength I pushed Tina to the ground and jumped on her. The gun was still in my hand.

"Cookie, this is dangerous. Don't let her get the gun," Charlotte said.

Tina was reaching for it, but luckily, I had her pinned down and she couldn't make contact with the weapon.

"Whew, that was a close call," Minnie said.

"I can't handle this stress," Charlotte said.

I wasn't sure what to do now. Should I keep her on the ground? Since I hadn't shot Tina she probably thought I wouldn't actually use the gun. I totally would if it was life or death.

I grabbed the back of Tina's shirt. "Okay, on your feet."

She climbed up from the ground.

"Place your hands on the car," I ordered with the gun pointed at her.

"This is just like the movies," Charlotte said.

"Yes, the movies with sound," Minnie said. "And in color."

"You thought you would get away from me, but I proved you wrong," I said.

"Don't get too cocky. The police haven't found you yet," Charlotte said.

Yes, I suppose I should save the gloating for a bit. What if the police didn't find me? The sirens could be headed somewhere else. Now what would I do? I couldn't stand here forever with my gun pointed at her. Eventually she would try to get away again.

"Do you have any plan for how to get her out of here?" Charlotte asked.

I shook my head.

"Oh dear," Minnie said.

It wasn't like I could put Tina in the car and drive her to the police station.

"Oh, I know. Make her walk toward the road and you can get service on that annoying contraption you call a telephone," Minnie said.

"Good idea, Minnie," I said.

"Leave it to me to be captured by a woman who talks to imaginary people," Tina said.

"Okay, with your hands in the air, turn around and start walking toward the main road," I ordered.

Tina didn't budge.

"You heard me," I yelled.

Charlotte and Minnie jumped. There was no need to carry out this plan though. Just as we turned around to head down the road I spotted the police cars speeding toward us.

"Thank goodness they made it." Charlotte sighed.

"I thought they'd never get here," Minnie said.

I'd kept it together, but my knees shook, as if I would collapse at any moment from the stress of what had happened. The police cars appeared speeding down the road toward us. Dylan's car was the first one in the line of many. He sped up to the scene and jumped out of the car with his gun drawn.

"You can put the gun down now, Cookie," Dylan said.

My hand shook as I lowered the weapon. After Dylan placed Tina in handcuffs, he escorted her into the backseat of the car. Maybe I shouldn't have hugged Dylan in front of the other officers, but I couldn't help it. I was just so grateful that all of this was over.

"Cookie, what are you doing out here?"

"What does it look like she's doing?" Charlotte asked. "She's catching a killer."

"Catching a killer," I said, trying to sound chipper.

Dylan wasn't buying the sweet and innocent act.

"You should have called me right away," Dylan said.

"There was no time. As soon as I saw her I took off."

"There was time to get Heather's car though?" Dylan asked with a quirked eyebrow.

"Well, I had to have a way to chase her," I said.

The police worked the scene for quite some time. Heather wouldn't be happy that her car was part of that crime scene. At least no one else had been hurt. Things had been touch and go there. I'd had no idea how I would get away from Tina. It was a good thing Minnie and Charlotte had used their energy to move the tree branch. It had been the perfect way to distract Tina. Thank goodness I'd been able to think quickly under pressure.

Charlotte was beside me, but Minnie wasn't there.

"Where's Minnie?" I asked.

Charlotte shrugged. "She was here a minute ago."

I looked around for Minnie, but she was nowhere in sight.

"Cookie, you can take Heather's car now," Dylan said as he approached. "No more chasing criminals though."

I smiled as I continued scanning the surroundings for Minnie.

"Is something wrong?" he asked.

"Minnie is gone."

"You mean she left?"

"I don't know. She would have said good-bye, right?"

"I'm not sure how the paranormal world portal works. Maybe she didn't have time."

I'd never thought of it that way. With other ghosts they'd always gotten a chance to say good-bye before they left. I suppose things could be different since Minnie said she was my guardian angel.

Dylan walked with me over to Heather's car. I

really didn't want to leave without Minnie. Dylan opened the car door and I noticed something on the driver's seat. It definitely hadn't been there before. The pearl necklace was on the seat of Heather's car.

I picked it up. Minnie's necklace. "Where is she?"

A piece of paper was also on the seat. I picked it up and unfolded it.

Dear Cookie,

I hoped that this time would come. The time when you didn't need my help. I enjoyed my time with you and Charlotte more than you'll ever know. I'll always be watching over you. If you need me again I'll be there. I'm bad at saying good-bye, so instead I'll say until I see you again.

Sincerely, Minnie.

P.S. Tell Charlotte not to pout. Someday if she's needed as a guardian angel she'll be able to use a pen too.

"She left a note," I said.

"What does it say?" Charlotte asked.

Dylan took the paper from my outstretched hand and read it. A smile slid across his face. Charlotte read the note from over Dylan's shoulder.

"I saw her writing a note the other day. How did she do that? It doesn't seem fair. She was being secretive," Charlotte said.

"Did you read the P.S.?"

Charlotte scanned to the bottom of the paper. "Oh. I suppose that's a good explanation."

"I guess so," I said around a sigh.

"Don't worry, Cookie, with your luck I'm sure you'll need her again soon." Charlotte laughed.

Dylan took the pearl necklace from my hand and clasped it around my neck. "I think she wanted you to have this."

"It's nice to know I have her watching out for me."

"Hey, what about me? I help you all the time." Charlotte placed her hands on her hips.

"You help me get in trouble," I said.

Chapter 25

*Look to vintage when shopping for
a wedding gown. Plus, your whole
wedding party can dress in vintage apparel.*

I'd gotten Heather's car back to her safely. Of course she'd freaked out when she heard what had happened. Not because her car had been in danger, but because I'd confronted a killer. Dylan had confirmed that Tina had stolen that black car and used it to make me wreck. Things were back to normal, although I still didn't have my car repaired. It had been two weeks since the accident. My guardian angel had left. Though I had a feeling Minnie Lynn would return if she was needed. Charlotte said she had a hunch that I would need Minnie Lynn again. She was probably right about that.

Now I had two cats hanging around the shop with me. My grandmother and Tyler. I enjoyed having them with me, but I also wanted them to move on to the next dimension if that was what was best for them. They didn't seem to be in a hurry to get there. So in the meantime I was looking more and more like the town's crazy cat lady. I was fine with that. My entire life I'd embraced being eccentric. I suppose my mother and I were more alike than I'd realized. We just had different ways of expressing it.

I was placing a 1960s cream color, beaded cardigan sweater on a hanger when Dylan walked through the door. I hadn't expected to see him this early. It was just now reaching lunchtime. My stomach did somersaults when I realized he was dressed in vintage. It was an outfit that I'd recently bought for him. He didn't wear vintage all the time, but occasionally he'd wear a shirt or slacks. He did it to make me happy, which was sweet. His black gabardine trousers had a four-pocket front pleat. His burgundy cotton shirt from the forties had pearl buttons along the front and cuffs with a fitted waist. His black steel-toe wing-tip loafers added the perfect final touch to his outfit.

"What's wrong with him?" Charlotte asked, eyeing Dylan up and down. "Though he does look dapper so we definitely shouldn't complain."

I wasn't sure what she meant until I took a closer look at his face. He was smiling, but there was something definitely off about the way he looked, almost as if he felt sick.

"Are you okay?" I asked, resisting the urge to reach out and touch his forehead to check for a fever.

He chuckled. "Of course. Why wouldn't I be okay?"

"Tell him because it looks as if he wants to throw up," Charlotte said.

His laugh was nervous too. Plus, he shifted from foot to foot as if he couldn't shake the jitters.

Dylan closed the distance between us. He took my hand in his. "I need you to come with me."

Now he was making me have the jitters. My stomach flipped.

"I don't have anyone to watch the store right now," I said.

"It's not as if it's busy right now," Charlotte said. "You can close for a bit."

The bell above the door chimed and Lynn walked toward me. My part-time employee never showed up early for work. Something was definitely wrong.

"Lynn, what are you doing here?" I asked. "You're not supposed to be here for a couple more hours."

"There's definitely something strange happening," Charlotte said.

"Lynn came in early so she can watch the shop for you," Dylan said with a smile.

"Okay, you're up to something," I said. "Is it my car? You have bad news about the Buick and you don't know how to break it to me?"

"Well, just go with him and find out what it is," Charlotte said with a wave of her hand. "If it's bad news it's better to find out now and get it over with."

Dylan took me by the hand and led me toward the door. "The cats have to come too. Come on, lady and gentleman."

The cats jumped down from the window and followed out the door. Charlotte was right behind us. I spotted Heather on the sidewalk. When she made eye contact with us she dashed back into her shop.

"What in the world? That is weird. Why are you all acting so strangely? You're beginning to worry me," I said.

What if this was more serious than the car? I'd spoken with my mother this morning and everything was fine with my parents.

"It's okay. Don't worry," Dylan said as he held my hand and guided me down the sidewalk.

Charlotte walked along beside us with the cats right behind. Traffic moved along at a steady pace up and down Main Street. Fluffy white clouds dotted the perfect blue sky. It was a beautiful day in Sugar Creek. Up ahead, I spotted a car.

"Is that my Buick?" My voice was louder than I'd intended, but I couldn't contain my excitement.

Surely there couldn't be another car just like mine in town. The car grew closer.

"That is my car. Quick, Dylan, someone stole my car. You have to go after them. Call for backup," I said in a panic.

I had spoken with the shop this morning, and they'd given no clue that the car was ready. They'd gotten used to daily calls from me. The car was special and I needed to check on it every day.

Dylan had no reaction to my panic. Why wasn't he saying anything? And why did he have that smile on his face? Movement to my right caught my attention.

Heather popped back out from her shop. Now she was dressed in vintage clothing. She never wore vintage. Even her hair was styled in victory rolls. Her dress was gold-quilted satin with a full circle skirt. The cap sleeves and pointed collar added to the charm of the piece. I was almost sure it was Dior.

Other people came out from shops, the diner, and around the corners from the side streets and alleyways. Everyone wore vintage clothing. I spotted my parents walking toward us. They were dressed in vintage too. Without even thinking, I let out a squeal of delight. My parents looked so good. Even my mother had left her hemp-infused clothing at home. She wore a yellow pencil skirt with a high waist that hit just below her knees. There was a slit in the front. Her short-sleeve white blouse had a pattern of tiny red and green flowers. I would be seriously impressed if she'd picked the outfit out.

"Did you plan all this?" I asked.

Dylan didn't answer, but the smile remained on his face. When I glanced over at Charlotte she was now wearing vintage.

"You too?"

She winked. Why was everyone being so tight-lipped?

Big band music streamed from the outdoor speakers around downtown Sugar Creek. It was as if I had been transported back in time. The cars that had traveled on the road earlier had disappeared. Now they were replaced by other vintage cars. My

Buick pulled up along the curb. It was shiny and perfect. Ken was behind the wheel. When he climbed out from behind the wheel I realized he was dressed in vintage too. Tears streamed down my cheeks.

Dylan lowered to the ground. Now he was on one knee. He pulled out a tiny black box and opened it. Inside was a gleaming diamond placed in a vintage gold setting. It was my grandmother's ring.

"Cookie Chanel, since the day I set eyes on you I knew you were special. I don't want to spend one single day of my life without you by my side. Will you marry me?" Dylan peered at me with his gorgeous blue eyes.

Sounds muted and all I saw was Dylan's handsome face peering up at me. From somewhere behind I thought I heard Charlotte screech with delight. Dylan was staring at me with his gorgeous blue eyes, waiting for an answer. This had come as a shock. I hadn't expected him to ask me to marry him. Sure, I'd thought about it. How could I not with Charlotte mentioning weddings all the time? Even my mother had mailed me wedding magazines. She'd set up a Pinterest board for items. Now the reality hit me. The future was here and I had to answer. I peered around at the smiling faces, though it looked as if they were getting nervous. Were they wondering if after Dylan went to all this effort I would say no?

"Yes, Dylan Valentine, I will marry you," I said.

"Cookie Valentine? Oh no. You must keep your

name," Charlotte said. "Cookie Chanel is much better."

Applause erupted around us. Dylan jumped up and swept me into his arms. He kissed me with passion like I'd never been kissed before. I couldn't believe this was happening. Everything still seemed so surreal. When we stopped the embrace I looked around at all the smiling faces. Everyone was still clapping and cheering.

"You planned all this?" I asked.

"For weeks now," Dylan said with a proud smile.

"I should have known this was coming. Well, I did, but not this soon," Charlotte said.

Heather and Ken walked over and hugged me. "Congratulations."

"You two were in on this. How long have you known?" I asked.

"A few weeks," Heather said. "It was hard to keep it a secret."

"Maybe they will be next," Charlotte said.

Wind Song meowed and I picked her up. "What do you say, Grandma Pearl? Will you be a bridesmaid?"

"Oh, now I've heard it all. A cat as a bridesmaid. I suppose that's appropriate for Cookie Chanel's wedding. Will Tyler be the best man? We have so much to do to prepare. I'm so excited." Charlotte paced around the sidewalk.

"Sweetheart, we're so happy for you. Dylan's

a lucky man to marry my daughter." My father wrapped his strong arms around me.

My mother brushed the hair from my face. "Oh, you can wear my wedding dress. I know you don't like the beads on it, but we can work something out."

Charlotte waved her arms. "Oh no. They're not having a hippie wedding in the back of some old VW van."

They were fighting already. I'd have to take control over this early on or they would be at each other's throats with me in the middle. Maybe I could make them compromise. I could remodel my mother's dress, and we could have the wedding venue at some fancy place that Charlotte liked.

"You've made me the happiest man alive," Dylan said, hugging me again.

I peered around at everyone dressed in their vintage fashion. "I can't believe everyone did this for me."

"It's the least we can do for Sugar Creek's finest detective," Dixie said. "Oh, and you too, Dylan."

Everyone laughed.

Turns out that Minnie Lynn wasn't murdered after all. She came back to earth only to help me. I kind of liked the idea of having a guardian angel. Now that I was safe, Minnie Lynn had left. I knew she was watching over me and saw Dylan propose. Charlotte was currently arguing she should be the maid of honor instead of Heather or Grandma Pearl. Ken had asked Heather to be his date for the wedding. Of course she said yes. I already knew I'd wear the pearl necklace that Minnie had left me.

Dylan had asked me to marry him, and I'd said yes. It was great to see happiness in Sugar Creek again. No more murders. At least I hoped there would be no more murders. I would be able to hang up my sleuthing hat once and for all.

BLOG POST *from* COOKIE CHANEL

Vintage Bags That Will Never Go Out of Style

Do you love designer handbags, but not the price tag that comes with them? Below I've listed styles that are still in fashion, but by buying vintage you can save a bundle. These handbags are classic and you can get them at a fraction of the cost of a new bag. Yet they look the same as the current style. Plus, I've listed handbag styles that are classic without the designer name. All of these handbags can make a casual outfit look glamorous or take a dressy ensemble to the next level. You can save thousands!

When spending this kind of money on a handbag it's a good idea to have it authenticated by a professional. You don't want to spend your money on something that's not the real deal. You're paying for the leather and craftsmanship. Plus, if you want to resell you'll have the peace of mind of knowing it's authentic.

1. The Louis Vuitton Speedy has been around since the 1930s. This handbag is made of coated canvas and has leather

handles, making it durable and water resistant. The style can take you from casual to dressy. It never goes out of style. Audrey Hepburn loved her Louis Vuitton Speedy.

2. Chanel Classic Flap Bag has several different versions. The bag can be worn as a cross body or over the shoulder. The chain strap adds a touch of jewelry to your outfit. The quality of caviar leather is almost as durable as the coated canvas of the Louis Vuitton Speedy. Coco Chanel designed the handbag in 1955 with what is referred to as the mademoiselle lock, but the signature CC lock version didn't come until the 1980s. The burgundy lining of the bag was inspired by the uniforms Coco wore in the orphanage where she grew up. Most bags have a double flap, but you might find some with a single flap.

3. Hermès has an air of exclusivity. Since each bag is handmade by one person and takes days to complete, that might explain some of the price tag. The Birkin, created for Jane Birkin in 1984, was designed as a travel bag with its two handles and wide opening. It has a classic structure and design. The Kelly bag was designed for Grace Kelly. It is chic with its single top handle. Whether you love the Birkin or Kelly they're both iconic.

4. The Gucci Jackie O Bag was named after First Lady Jackie Kennedy Onassis. The bag was released in the 1950s, but was renamed in 1961. Whether in the signature logo or luxurious leather, the slouchy shape still has structure making this hobo style shoulder bag a timeless piece.

5. The Lady Dior bag was renamed for Princess Diana. This handmade leather handbag debuted in 1994, but was renamed in 1996. Princess Diana loved this bag and ordered one in every color. The bag has padded stitched leather and a letter charm that spells Dior.

6. Classic style handbags don't have to have a designer name. Styles to look for are tote, cross body, and satchel. You can get a similar look to the above-mentioned bags without investing the cost. Look for quality well-made pieces that will last you for years to come.

ACKNOWLEDGMENTS

Thank you to my mother for introducing me to the wonderful world of books.

Thank you to my husband for encouraging me, always having faith in me, and always being there for me. Huge thank-yous to my editor, Michaela Hamilton, and my agent, Jill Marsal, for all the help in making this series possible.

Announcing an irresistible new cozy mystery
series by beloved author
ROSE PRESSEY,
coming soon from Kensington Publishing Corp.!

THE HAUNTED ARTS AND CRAFT mystery series
will feature the sleuthing adventures of
Celeste Cabot, an artist who travels the South
in her sweet pink and white Shasta trailer
with her four-pound white Chihuahua,
Vincent van Gogh, as she sells her paintings
and solves murders.
Keep reading to enjoy an excerpt from

Murder Can Mess Up
Your Masterpiece

Chapter 1

"I want to return this horrible painting." The tall, willowy gray-haired woman placed the canvas down on the table in front of me.

Yesterday, when she'd purchased the art piece from me, she'd been impeccably dressed and practically flawless. Today she was a hot mess. Her hair tumbled around her flushed face and dark circles colored under her icy blue eyes. Her white blouse and navy blue trousers were the same she'd worn the day before, but were now in desperate need of an iron, as if she'd slept in the clothing. Who was I to notice such things though? My outfit was worse. I peered down at my paint-stained jeans. Various colors decorated the front of my white T-shirt too.

This was day two of the four-day annual Summer Arts and Craft Fair in my hometown of Gatlinburg, Tennessee. Selling my art was my full-time job now, so having one return would hurt my already too-tight budget.

My art display was set up in vendor spot number forty-one. Behind me was my fabulous pink and white Shasta trailer. The adorable little thing would be my home away from home now. I planned on spending a lot of time in the tiny trailer as I traveled the country, bringing my art to each and every state.

"Is there something wrong with the painting?" I asked.

She placed her hands on her slender hips. "Is there something wrong?" Now she was mocking me. "Yes, you could say that something is wrong."

My four-pound white Chihuahua, Vincent van Gogh, yipped at the woman as he wiggled in my arms. He acted as if he wanted down so he could chase her away. In reality he would run and hide in the trailer. I called him Van for short. She glared at him. He wouldn't bite her unless she tried to pet him. Or if she turned her back and I let him down. Van had been protective of me since the day I'd rescued him from the animal shelter. One of his giant ears flopped down and that was how he'd gotten the name van Gogh.

Claiming that she had changed her mind wouldn't be a good enough reason for a return, in my opinion, but what else could be the problem? If she didn't want it I would have to give her the money back.

"What seems to be the problem?" I used the sweetest tone possible.

I'd never forget the evening I painted the aforementioned piece of art. Rain had battered against the windows of my tiny cottage, almost in rhythm with each stroke of my brush. Thunder rattled the walls and the lightning had caused the lights to flicker on and off. The dense trees surrounding my place acted almost as a comforting earthy embrace. While at home I always felt safe from the overwhelming and hectic world.

Oil paint was my preferred medium that brought the portrait to life. The subject of my work had popped into my mind as clear as any living person. It was as if she was pleading with me to immortalize her on the canvas. I had no idea who she was, but I knew her beauty had to be captured. She wore an ornately trimmed red and gold Victorian-era gown with her dark hair pulled up into a French twist. That was exactly how I depicted her in the portrait.

"The painting is haunted," the woman said without batting an eyelash.

I glanced around to see if anyone else was in on this joke. Fairgoers milled around the grounds with other artists selling their wares. No one was paying attention to me or my disgruntled customer.

"Did Evan put you up to this?" I asked around a laugh.

The lines between her stone-cold eyes deepened. "I don't know Evan. Frankly, I'm insulted that you would accuse me of anything that devious."

Uh-oh. Now I was riling her up even more. Apparently she was completely serious. She was a few strokes short of a finished portrait.

"Why do you think the painting is haunted?" Curiosity forced me to ask this question.

"Right after I took it home, strange things started happening. Things that had never happened before, so I knew it had to be this painting causing the chaos." She gestured toward the canvas.

I frowned. "What type of strange things?"

She tossed her hands up in frustration. "Doors slamming, unexplained footsteps, and the painting was knocked off the wall and landed on the floor all the way across the room."

That sounded like something out of a scary movie. Still, I had my doubts that this woman was telling the truth. I didn't believe in ghosts.

Grabbing my bag, I pulled out the cash that she had given me less than twenty-four hours ago. "Here you are. One hundred dollars."

It pained me to let go of the money. I had big plans for those bills—like buying food.

She counted the twenties to make sure I hadn't stiffed her. What kind of operation did she think I was running? After all, she was the one who thought the painting was haunted. What a crazy idea. I pushed my shoulders back and held my head high. It would be all right. Another buyer would come along who appreciated my work.

I wanted to ask her more about this "haunting," but then I thought better of it. Clearly, she was just making this up in order to return the painting. Plus, even if I changed my mind and decided to ask, it wasn't an option now. She turned and hurried away before another word was exchanged. At

least that tête-à-tête was over, and now I could go
back to work.

After placing the painting back on the easel next
to the other canvases, I picked up my brush to add
a little more detail to my current project. While I
waited for other customers to come by I painted.
I'd done fairly well at this show so far, selling four
paintings in just one day. The rest of the weekend
was ahead of me, and with any luck I'd sell even
more. My fingers were crossed that I wouldn't re-
ceive another return.

This time I was working on a portrait of a young
woman and her horse. The inspiration had come
from a woman I'd seen riding at a nearby farm. I
thought it would make a lovely painting. Now I was
creating it from memory.

For most of my paintings I used oil paint. In my
opinion the oil made it easier to get just the right
look. My interest in art started at the age of four-
teen. It was hard to believe that had been twenty
years ago now. The only time I'd had any art train-
ing was a class in seventh grade and then again in
high school. I'd never made it to college. Things
had come up that prevented me from attending—
things like no money. I'd taken a job at the local
thrift shop and worked there up until two weeks
ago. I figured sixteen years was enough and it was
time for a change.

"I'm quite impressed by your work." The female
voice snapped my attention away from the colors in
front of me.

The dark-haired woman studied the canvas. It was the portrait that the other woman had just returned. A potential new customer? Could I get that lucky? The woman was even shorter than me at probably five feet. Her long straight hair reached past her waist. In some ways she reminded me of my mother. They were probably close to the same age. Everyone said I looked a lot like my mother with dark hair and big brown eyes the shade of a scrumptious piece of Godiva chocolate.

"Thank you," I said, putting down my brush.

Her comment was just the boost I had needed after the earlier encounter with the unhappy customer.

The woman studied the portrait through her thick black eyeglasses. "Did you add the skull in her dress on purpose?"

I frowned. "I'm sorry. What do you mean?"

She pointed. "On the woman's dress there's a skull. It's an interesting touch. Quite haunting."

I moved around the table and now stood beside her, staring at the portrait. Still I couldn't see the skull. Was she just as nutty as the other customer?

"You don't see it, do you?" she asked.

"No, I'm sorry."

She removed her eyeglasses and examined the portrait again. "That's odd. When I look at it without my glasses it's not there."

"Maybe there's a reflection or smear on your glasses," I said.

After wiping them with the edge of her shirt she placed them back on her face. "It's still there."

I wasn't quite sure what to say.

She removed the eyeglasses once again. "Here, you put them on and tell me what you see."

This was the second odd experience that I'd had in less than an hour. My life had always been uneventful. Apparently, I was making up for that now. Nonetheless, I took the frames and put them on as she'd asked. Whoa, I'd get a headache quickly wearing them. Once my eyes adjusted, I peered at the portrait. It was exactly as she'd described.

"Do you see it?" she asked excitedly.

"I see it now. I never painted that. At least not on purpose."

"Maybe it was just a trick of the strokes," she said.

"I'm sure no other paintings would have this."

Keeping her eyeglasses on, I moved to the right a couple steps. Peering at another painting, I couldn't believe my eyes. Another image was in this painting. This time it was a skeleton, not just a skull. A shiver ran down my spine. I pulled the eyeglasses off.

"What do you see?" the woman asked.

The skeleton wasn't visible without the eyeglasses. I handed them back to her.

"It's a skeleton." My voice was barely above a whisper.

She put on the glasses and studied the painting. "Oh, I see it too. You didn't do that on purpose? That's amazing. You have such talent."

I shook my head no, still in shock. The woman stepped around me to examine the other artwork I had on display. "Oh, there's a hidden image in all of them."

I couldn't wrap my mind around how this had happened. If it had occurred only once I would think it was a fluke, but that couldn't be the case when it occurred in all of them. Was it just her eyeglasses? Yes, that had to be the case. This was another joke. The woman claiming the painting was haunted was a joke, and now someone was playing another trick on me. I wanted to know who the prankster was.

"Who put you up to this?" I asked.

She furrowed her brow. "I don't know what you're implying, but I'm not fooling around. I have the booth two down from you. I make jewelry."

I glanced down the lane at her table full of jewelry on display.

"I'm sorry, but it has to be your eyeglasses," I said.

"Do you have anything else glass?" she asked.

"I have a jar that I use to clean my brushes." I gestured.

"I wonder if you could see the image through that too? Or if it has to be magnified?"

I rushed over and retrieved the jar. Lifting it up to my face, I peered through the glass at the painting. A gasp escaped my mouth when I spotted the skull.

"See? I told you it wasn't my eyeglasses. You should

be happy. This is a true talent and a work of art. Embrace it." She patted me on the back.

Moving from painting to painting, I examined each one. They all featured some kind of hidden image. I suppose I had to believe it now since I was seeing it with my own eyes. How did this happen? I hadn't planned it. I suppose I had painted the images with my subconscious.

"My name's Dorothy Gordon, by the way." She stretched her hand out toward me.

I shook her hand. "Celeste Cabot. Nice to meet you."

"Are you okay? I still can't believe you didn't know about this."

"No idea," I said, still eyeing the painting.

The more I looked at the woman in the portrait, the more I noticed her eyes. They seemed different now somehow, but I couldn't put my finger on why I thought that. The sound of a motor caught my attention. Evan Wright, the man in charge of setting up the craft fair, was driving a golf cart down the path in front of our booths. At six-foot-three with wide shoulders and a hefty stature, he barely fit behind the wheel of that tiny vehicle.

"Good morning, ladies. Not having any luck with selling your wares, I see." His loud boisterous laugh carried across the summer air.

Evan didn't wait around for an answer. He punched the pedal, jerking his head backward. His laughter continued as he drove off.

"I don't like that guy," Dorothy said with disdain in her voice.

"He's not pleasant, is he?" I asked.

"I've overheard quite a few vendors talk about how much they don't like him. As a matter of fact, I might not come back next year if he's still here."

"I certainly understand why you feel that way," I said. "Like my grandma always says, he's as useful as a pogo stick in quicksand."

"Oh, it looks as if I have customers. It was nice meeting you, Celeste." She tossed her hand up in a wave and rushed away to help the customers.

Now I was alone, staring at the woman's portrait. Or was she staring at me?

Connect with Us

Visit us online at
KensingtonBooks.com
to read more from your favorite authors, see books
by series, view reading group guides, and more.

for sneak peeks, chances to win books and prize packs,
and to share your thoughts with other readers.

facebook.com/kensingtonpublishing
twitter.com/kensingtonbooks

Tell us what you think!

To share your thoughts, submit a review,
or sign up for our eNewsletters, please visit:
KensingtonBooks.com/TellUs.